Daliah

A Needful Bride

Danni Roan

ISBN-10:1089341229
ISBN-13 : 978-1089341222
ISBN-10: 1477123456

Cover design by: Erin Dameron-Hill
Library of Congress Control Number: 2018675309
Printed in the United States of America

A man's heart deviseth his way: but the LORD directeth his steps.
Proverbs: 16:9
KING JAMES BIBLE

Contents

Chapter 1

"Miss Owens, if I could see you in my office, please," Mr. Bradford, the bank president, motioned Daliah to his open door.

"Yes, sir," Daliah was quick to comply, she'd been working at the Smithfield bank for nearly two years, and aside from her interview, she didn't believe she'd ever said more than 'good day,' to the bank president.

"Please take a seat," Mr. Bradford said, indicating a chair before his oversized mahogany desk.

Daliah slipped into the proffered chair, nervously toying with the lace at her collar. It had been a hard sell for her taking over her brother's job at the bank when he'd been killed by the crossfire of a botched bank robbery. With no prospects of making it on her own without her brother, she'd done the only thing she could think of and had practically begged the wealthy businessman for her brother's job.

"Is something wrong, Mr. Bradford?" Daliah finally asked as the rather rotund banker settled onto his chair with a protesting screech.

"I'm afraid that your till has come up short," Mr. Bradford said, looking at her over his wire-rimmed spectacles. "This is highly irregular," he continued. "Mr. Shaw, our new manager, has advised me that your drawer has been nearly two dollars short twice this month."

Daliah's mouth fell open in horror. "I assure you, Mr. Bradford, when I returned my drawer to the safe each evening, my numbers tallied perfectly." How could she be short when she'd kept impeccable records, turning them over each day to the new bank manager?

"Miss Owens, this sort of thing cannot be overlooked. I know you've been a stellar employee to date, but if there's some problem, some need at home, perhaps we could work something out." Mr. Bradford's expression was firm but not unkind, and it made Daliah squirm.

"Surely you can't believe that I've shorted the bank on any transaction," she protested. "I've never had so much as a penny go wrong in two years."

"Mistakes do happen," Mr. Bradford suggested, "but Mr. Shaw was very adamant that you have been short twice."

Daliah shook her head, "I'll fetch my records," she suggested rising to her feet.

"No need for that," Mr. Bradford said, dismissing the thought with a wave of his hand. "I've already seen them." He tapped a pile of neat papers on the end of his desk. "Now, do you have anything to tell me?" He asked again.

"Mr. Bradford," Daliah said, feeling the blood rush to her face as her heart began to pound. "My drawer has never been short. There has to be a mistake."

"Miss Owens, perhaps if you could explain the circumstances that have brought you to this desperate measure, we could work something out."

"Circumstances?" Daliah gaped.

"Yes, I know how hard it has been for you since your brother passed. I only gave you this position because he had been such a wonderful asset to the bank. With your parents gone and then losing your brother, I thought it only fair to give you a chance, but if this is how you repay my benevolence...."

He let the words drift away as his dark eyes tried to peer through her.

"Mr. Bradford, are you accusing me of stealing from the bank?" Daliah asked, her voice shaking.

"I wouldn't put it that way, but there have been these two irregularities."

Daliah felt the world spinning out of control. "If I might see my ledger please?" she asked, reaching out a hand toward the papers on Mr. Bradford's desk.

"Mr. Shaw and I have been through every page, my dear; you are exactly four dollars and seventy-four cents short this month. That's more than some men make as wages in a week. I'm afraid that if you are not willing to confess and explain why you have kept back that amount, I have no choice but to let you go."

"But I didn't do it," Daliah wailed, rising to her feet, "I've never had a single coin go astray, and now I'm being accused of stealing. This isn't right. It isn't fair."

"Miss Owens, if you are determined to make a scene, I could call the sheriff. As it is, I have decided to dismiss you without reference out of my affection for your late brother. If you'll please gather your things, I'll see you out."

Daliah rose, clutching her bag and fighting back the tears. She couldn't understand what was happening. She'd been a diligent employee for two years. Not only was this her only means of support, but it was also her joy in a job well done. She'd even been of help to those less educated in sums and numbers in the community, many of whom asked for her regularly.

Mr. Bradford was opening the door and the bright light of day dazzled her making her blink. "I'm sorry about this whole mess, Miss Owens," the banker was saying with a shake of his head. "If you have anything else to say?" he finished hopefully.

Daliah shook her head as she stepped through the door. What could she say? She had no idea what had happened or where the lost funds could have gone. With no argument left, the young woman stumbled toward the home where she rented a tiny room from an elderly couple.

***

"Daliah, my dear, what are you doing home so early? Are you feeling well?" Mrs. Hampton hurried to the door as Daliah stepped through. "You aren't getting ill, are you?" the older woman asked, reaching out to feel the girl's forehead.

Daliah shook her head as the tears she'd been fighting the whole way home began to flow. "I lost my job," she sobbed, letting Mrs. Hampton guide her to a chair in the kitchen.

"Sit here, dear," Mrs. Hampton said, pulling a handkerchief from her sleeve and handing it to her young boarder. "I'll make us a cup of tea and you tell me what happened."

Daliah poured out her heart to the slim gray-haired woman as she struggled to understand what had happened and to figure out what she would do now that she had no job. Surely others would hear of her shame and what reputable business would hire her after she had dismissed her from the bank. Mr. Bradford would be forced to tell any prospective employer why she'd been let go, and no one would ever hire her. With a moan, she laid her head on the table and sobbed.

"Daliah Owens, you sit up and drink your tea now," Mrs. Hampton said, her harsh words making Daliah jump. "This is a terrible thing, it is, but it ain't the end of the world. We'll figure out something, and God will see you through." Olive Hampton patted the girl's back as she placed the cup on the table.

Daliah took the tea cup in shaking hands and sipped the sweet hot brew. She needed to pull herself together. Sitting and blubbering about her situation wouldn't fix it, and she didn't have a soul in the world she could count on to sort it out for her.

"You've been through worse than this now," Mrs. Hampton said, taking a seat and patting her on the arm. "When your folks were killed along the trail to Missouri, you and your brother managed, and when you lost your dear brother, you found a job and a place to stay. I know God must have a plan, even if others are the ones making things bad for you."

Daliah looked up into the narrow face of the

woman who had taken her in when she had nowhere to go and tried to smile.

"I don't know what I'll do, Mrs. Hampton," she said. "At least when Joe and I arrived here in Smithfield, he was able to get a job and look out for us, even after..." she hiccupped softly, dabbing at her eyes, "even after I lost Joe, I had my reputation as an honest worker."

Mrs. Hampton nodded and listened as Daliah worked through the issues, a keen light shining in her eyes.

"We'll wait until Orville gets home," Mrs. Hampton finally said, "and then we'll see. I'm sure he'll have a few ideas of his own."

Daliah nodded. Orville Hampton was well known and well-liked in Smithfield. He'd owned and operated the sawmill that had practically built the town, and even now, as age and physical limitation prevented him from working such long hours, many looked up to him as a pillar of the city.

"Now, you go wash your face and hands and say your prayers," Mrs. Hampton said, picking up their empty cups and turning to the sink. "We'll discuss everything over dinner tonight."

Daliah rose, feeling slightly encouraged by the older woman's sage words and tripping to her bedroom. She did as she was told, whispering prayers for help along the way.

Chapter 2

"Orville, it would be the chance we've been wait-ing for," Mrs. Hampton's voice drifted to Daliah as she made her way back to the kitchen sometime later.

"I reckon it'd work all right," the old man mused.

Daliah wasn't sure how old Mr. Hampton was, but he seemed ancient to her twenty years. She knew he'd been with the town sawmill for nearly thirty years before turning it over to his sons.

"It'd be the start you wanted and think of the country we'd see; besides talk has it there'll be a railroad through soon." Mrs. Hampton continued, stopping only when she saw Daliah enter the room.

"Is everything all right?" Daliah asked, noting the silence.

"Sit down, dear," Mrs. Hampton said. "I'll get our dinner."

Daliah didn't argue. She could see that Mrs. Hampton had something on her mind and knew that it was better to go along until she understood what was expected of her.

"Ma was telling me about your trouble Daliah," Mr. Hampton said. He shook his head, making his mane of white hair fall over his eyes. "Bad business, bad business," he continued. "Mr. Bradford is out of line, but naught we can do about it."

Daliah nodded, appreciating the man's kind words.

"Seems a fresh start would be the best thing," Mr. Hampton finished as his wife placed a Dutch oven of baked chicken and vegetables on the table.

"Pa and me was talking," the lady of the house said, "and we thought starting out with a wagon train might be a plan. There's a small group headed to Texas soon, ya see."

Daliah looked between the two of them, confused. "I can't afford to move."

"No, but we can," Mr. Hampton said with a smile as he reached out to take their hands and offer up grace.

When the Amen was said, Daliah looked up to her host expectantly.

"Orville and I have been talking about a new start for a while now." Mrs. Hampton said.

"I always wanted to see more of this land," Orville spoke up. "I came out here and started my mill, raised a family, had a life, but I haven't seen so much as I'd like."

"We know we ain't young, but if you'd go along with us, we'd manage just fine. One of the boys can see to the house and we can get a wagon easy enough."

"I can't ask you to do that," Daliah argued, toying with her food. "This is your home. Your family is here. There must be another way."

"We don't want another way," Mrs. Hampton said, pursing her lips. "We want to go out and see something new. It'll be an adventure."

Daliah looked at the older couple again. Neither were young, though they didn't have any serious health issues. How could they possibly want to move out of their home?

"There's a wagon train leaving in three weeks," Mr. Hampton said. "If we get everything together, we can head south with them. I hear some areas down there are still as wild as ever."

Daliah squirmed in her chair. Everything was happening way too fast. Surely it would be better if she stayed and tried to clear up the issue at the bank. Wouldn't it look suspicious if she left?

"Don't you go over thinking this now, dear," Mr. Hampton said. "Folks will just think you left because you were traveling with us."

"Honey, it would be a new start," Mrs. Hampton said, taking Daliah's hand. "It would let us live out a dream we've had for years and give you a new beginning. Say yes."

A warm wave seemed to pass over Daliah as she sat at the table and a flicker of hope ignited in her heart.

"Do you think it would be all right?" Daliah asked. "What will people think?"

"Folks is gonna think what they will," Mrs. Hampton said. "You can't change that. You just gotta do what you know is right in your heart."

"I do have a little saved," Daliah said. "I can help out with supplies, and you know I'll work hard," a hint of excitement quivered in her middle.

Smithfield had been her home for nearly five years, yet it had never felt like one. Her parents had decided to move their family west but had died of a fever on their way to Missouri and the starting point of the westward trails.

Daliah and her brother had managed to make a life, eking out a living before Joe had gotten a job at the bank and was killed in a botched robbery. Smithfield had been a town that had brought her great sorrow. Could she leave it all behind and start over? It seemed like a chance that would be worth taking.

Orville Hampton looked at his wife and winked. "I'll go speak with York at the livery after dinner," he said smiling, "looks like we're up for an adventure." He turned, looking toward Daliah. "It'll work out. You just wait and see."

Daliah let a slow smile spread across her face. She'd returned to the tiny home with her heart in her shoes, but now she felt that she might have a chance at something new.

Chapter 3

Over the next few weeks, Daliah was kept so busy preparing for the spring rollout that she hardly had time to think about her unfortunate circumstance.

Mr. Hampton had lists of things for her to do, items for her to buy, and then Mrs. Hampton had a thousand and one things to sort through and pack.

They'd already packed the necessary utensils at least three times, and Daliah was sure they'd probably pack them at least three more times again as Mrs. Hampton remembered just one more thing she still needed.

"We'll need the big Dutch oven," Mrs. Hampton called as she rummaged under the copper sink, her skirts swishing with the curtains that covered the space.

"I'll get it," Daliah called back, not wanting the older woman to have to carry the cast-iron pot.

"You women 'bout sorted?" Mr. Hampton walked into the kitchen, freezing Daliah on the spot. He was wearing a wide-brimmed hat and heavy boots over denims and looked like a penny dreadful wanna-be.

"Don't you look like the bee's knees," Mrs. Hampton said, backing herself out from the storage space on all fours and settling on her bottom. "Give me a hand up, Orville," she finished waggling her hands.

Orville hurried to his wife, who smiled at him the way he liked as he grasped her hands, pulling and tugging until she'd found her feet.

"I'm not as agile as I once was," Mrs. Hampton said, "but I get by with a little help."

Orville leaned over and kissed her wrinkled cheek, making Daliah smile. What devotion the two had to each other, and even when others thought they must be crazy, packing up a lifetime and heading out into the unknown, they stuck together.

Did people still love like that, she wondered? Were there men who were truly steadfast, honorable, and devoted? Unfortunately, she'd seen little evidence of it recently, and after the heart-wrenching debacle at the bank, doubted she'd be able to trust any man other than Mr. Hampton to hold sway over her existence.

"Go fetch the kettle," Mrs. Hampton said, placing the long wooden spoon she'd just retrieved into a crate. "I think that just about does it." She finished looking up at her husband. "Have the boys decided we're not completely stark raving mad yet?" she asked with a twinkle.

"They've come to accept what we're doing," Orville said, "don't like it much, but they'll live with it. I might 'a told them the rail was coming, and we could be back in no time if we chose," he added, with a grin.

"I will miss the children," Olive Hampton said, "but we can always come back if this isn't any good," she finished placing her hands on his stubbly chin and kissing him softly.

***

Daliah looked at her meager possessions, examining each item with care to determine if she couldn't live without anything.

She had her mother's locket, father's watch, and brother's gold chain tucked into a leather sack and tied up tight to protect them from prying eyes and the elements.

She had two extra, serviceable dresses, two nightgowns, three changes of undergarments, and an extra pair of boots. Quietly, she ran her hands over the lovely dress that had been her mother's, debating whether she should keep it, then folded it and stuffed it into the bottom of her bag.

Next, she eyed the battered round-topped hat that had been her brothers. It was a good hat that would keep the weather off as they trekked westward, but it wasn't ladylike. She knew that most women would be wearing sensible bonnets.

Stepping to the mirror, she pulled the hat on over her intricately braided golden hair.

"You look like a boy," she chided herself, adjusting the hat and examining her narrow face in the mirror. She had nothing memorable in her looks, but her usual smile won friends at least most of the time.

"Daliah," Mrs. Hampton's voice drifted down the hall. "Dinner's almost ready."

Daliah hurried back to her bed and began packing everything into a canvas bag. Mr. Hampton had been moving supplies to the wagon he'd purchased all week and in one more day, they would be leaving Smithfield forever. Tucking the tiny tintype photo of her parents into the smaller leather bag, she hurried to the kitchen to help with the meal.

Daliah stopped at the end of the hall in shock as a tall man stepped through the front door, removing his hat from a head of shimmering chestnut hair while his other hand held to a boy's arm.

Mr. Hampton, who was holding the door, offered his hand. "Mr. Gaines, so glad you could make it. I appreciated your help with the wagon and wanted to thank you with a proper meal before we leave."

"I'm obliged," Mr. Gaines spoke, his eyes traveling the small space and coming to rest on Daliah standing in the hall.

"This is Daliah Owens, our boarder," Mr. Hampton offered, closing the door and gesturing Daliah into the room. "Daliah's going with us to see that these crazy old folks can manage," he added with a smile. "It's one of the reasons our children aren't having too much of a fit."

"Pleased to meet you," Daliah said, smiling at the boy but noting the harsh look on the man's face as his eyes traveled to her head.

She'd completely forgotten she was wearing her brother's hat and quickly hurried to take it off, unveiling her golden locks. "I'm sorry I forgot all about that," she blushed. "It was my brother's."

"Gimmee, gimme," the little boy said, breaking loose of his father's hand and snatching the hat from Daliah's hands. Daliah gasped as the boy squashed the hat onto his head, covering nearly half of his face at the same time.

"This is Chad," Mr. Gaines spoke. His voice was deep and resonant, like a warm drink on a cold day. "Give that back, Chad."

The boy of about five shook his head, making the hat dance and swivel.

"It's not yours, so give it back," he said more harshly.

Slowly the boy pulled the hat off of his head and handed it back to Daliah, who thanked him sweetly. "I'll just put this up," she said awkwardly, feeling flustered as she hurried back to her room, where she quickly combed out her hair and fastened it into a respectable knot at the back of her neck.

Smoothing her skirts, she took a deep breath and headed back to the kitchen. As first impressions went, her first meeting with Mr. Gaines, a man she would be traveling with, had not gone well. She hoped that the second would be better.

Smiling brightly, Daliah entered the kitchen, moving quickly to help Mrs. Hampton finish dinner. The older woman had done her best to cook a feast, claiming that they might as well eat up perishables that they couldn't take with them as let it go to waste.

Both women gasped and turned as a loud clatter

of cutlery echoed through the room and their eyes fell on the little boy who stood grinning at the pile of silverware he'd dumped onto the floor.

"Chad, don't do that," Mr. Gaines barked, heading to the boy just as Daliah reached him and began picking up the mess.

"It's all right," she said. "I'll just wash them, and then we'll eat" Her eyes met his and for a moment, all the air seemed to leave the room as her chest grew tight. He was a very handsome man.

"Chad, you sit down," the man growled, "I'll clean this up." His hard eyes bore into Daliah as if expecting her to argue, but she didn't. Instead, she smiled and helped the boy into a chair.

"Are you hungry?" she asked and the boy nodded, swiping a sleeve under his nose with a sniff which Daliah ignored. "Mrs. Hampton is a very good cook, and I'm sure you'll like what she makes. I heard something about pie for dessert if we eat all of our dinner," she added, noting the way the boy's eyes lit up.

The clatter of cutlery in the sink made Daliah cringe as she settled the boy and poured him a glass of milk. "Let me just help your father, and then we'll eat."

Rolling up her sleeves, Daliah stepped up to the

taciturn man. "I think it best if I finish this," she said pointedly.

"Spencer, you come on over here and get out of the way," Mr. Hampton called as he took a seat at the small table. "Olive don't like me in her kitchen, so's you'd best move."

Spencer Gaines looked down at the pert young woman next to him and nodded, stepping away from the sink where she was pumping water. He had no place in a kitchen and he knew it. He was more at home out on the prairie or traveling. If his brother hadn't asked him to come to Texas, he probably would have been looking toward Oregon or California.

He looked down at his son, now sitting at the table listening to a story Mr. Hampton was telling. The scamp was always into something. The boy had a knack for finding trouble. It wasn't going to be easy keeping an eye on him on the drive to Texas. But, at least once they got there, the boy would have plenty of room to grow.

Mrs. Hampton turned, placing a plate of roast beef and vegetables on the table, then turned back to the stove for biscuits. The smells were making his mouth water. He'd jumped at the chance for a good dinner when Mr. Hampton invited him. The older man was a cheerful sort and seemed determined to go on this trip.

Spencer looked up as the young woman, Daliah, her name was, placed a fork and knife at his elbow with a smile. He thanked her politely but hoped the girl would stay out of his way in the long run. He had no room for women in his life after losing his wife.

Chapter 4

Excitement filled the air as wagons rolled into line on the outskirts of town one by one. It was a small wagon train headed for Texas on rumors that there was a need for people in the Lone Star state after the war.

Mr. Hampton, his wife, perched on the bench seat next to him, pulled his team of fine horses to a stop at the back of the line and waited for Daliah to climb out of the wagon bed.

"You got everything stowed?" Mrs. Hampton asked, her cheeks rosy with the thrill of finally starting out.

"Yes, nothing seems to have wiggled loose on the short drive. I think we're squared away."

"I hope we have enough?" Mrs. Hampton mused.

"I hope we don't have too much," Mr. Hampton grumped.

The banter between the two always made Daliah smile. She was happy to be leaving Smithfield and all of its unpleasant memories behind. A new start was what she needed. She hoped that others wouldn't see it as her running away. Quietly, she looked toward the blue skies above and whispered a prayer for the journey.

Mr. Gaines trotted up along the wagons, checking in with each family, Chad seated on the saddle in front of his father, his little face sticky from a sweet he was eating.

"Mr. Hampton, Mrs. Hampton," Spencer greeted as he pulled up next to their wagon. He'd put them at the end of the train in a position to move slowly. Mr. Hampton had one of the best teams in the train. The majority of the travelers had oxen, and this way, Mr. Hampton wouldn't need to keep slowing his team but could meander along behind the line of wagons at his own pace.

From the corner of his eye, Spencer saw the young woman pull her floppy wide-brimmed hat onto her head and had to smile. It wasn't conventional, but he liked her determination to wear the hat in honor of her brother just the same.

"Wagon's Ho!" echoed down the line from his partner in this endeavor and Spencer turned his horse back toward the front of the line, wrapping and an arm around his son and galloping toward the quiet gray-haired leader that everyone called Ben. It was time to get moving.

***

"Pa, how's come that one woman wears a funny hat?" Chad asked as he held to the saddle horn along the trail.

"I think it has some sentimental value to her or something," Spencer replied, scanning the horizon for signs of their first stopping point.

It was early spring and the weather, though cold, was fine and clear of any snow. The journey looked promising to start at least. For Spencer, this would be his final trial. His brother had written telling him that the tiny town where he lived had plenty of land and hope to offer.

"What's semi-mental mean?" the boy asked, making Spencer chuckle. Even with his mischievous ways, the boy could always make him smile. "Sentimental, it means it has feelings attached to it. Something she cares about because of her memories," Spencer said.

"Like my blanket mama made," Chad said, nodding his understanding.

Spencer swallowed down the anger in his chest and nodded. "Yes, like the blanket your mama made you." He didn't like to think of his late wife. Even after three years, he felt the sharp pain of loss. Rebecca had been a good wife and a good mother, but she had not had the strength to survive pneumonia.

Since her death, Spencer had found it hard to settle anywhere. He'd moved Chad five times in the past three years, each time growing discontent with his situation and moving on. Several times, he took on a trail drive or led a wagon train for sections of a trail while his son stayed behind with family or friends.

Perhaps Texas would be the answer. Maybe he'd find a place where he could finally put his aching heart to rest. His brother Dan felt it was the right move. Having family about might even make settling down more manageable.

"Pa, you think if I offer to help that lady, I might get another slice of pie when we stop tonight?" Chad asked hopefully.

"You leave those folks alone," Spencer chided. "You're not their responsibility." He didn't know how he would keep the boy out of trouble on the long drive, but he also wanted to avoid the rather attractive young woman traveling with the Hamptons.

The boy turned his dirty face up to look at his father but didn't say anything. However, Spencer knew that his word was not the end of the boy's thoughts on the matter.

As the wagon train spread out across the plains, Spencer tried to settle his mind. It had largely been his idea to travel south. He'd mentioned it to a few people in town and soon, he'd gathered nine families with wagons for the train.

Most of the group was made up of people who didn't want to, or couldn't afford to, make the trail to Oregon and were eager to see if Texas was where they belonged. Spencer looked forward to seeing more of the land. He only wished he'd have some time to let Chad down to play.

Evening came quickly, and Spencer was glad when Mrs. Hampton offered to take Chad while he rode the camp checking in on others. He knew the boy would be well fed and hopefully stay out of trouble. He'd probably eat with the Hamptons as well, seeing that their fire was at the edge of camp.

When Spencer returned to the Hampton wagon, the first thing he noticed was his son enjoying a thick piece of leftover pie with the younger woman of the group. He shook his head even as his stomach grumbled while he swung down from the saddle, heading for the fire.

"You're just in time for dinner," Mr. Hampton said, handing the man a plate. "You finish that up and Daliah might even have a piece of pie left for you too. She makes a mighty nice pie."

Daliah turned at her name, seeing Mr. Gaines look up with a smile that caught her by surprise. He didn't seem the sort who smiled often.

"I'm all done," Chad said, looking up from the bucket where he'd been washing his hands as she'd instructed. "Can I go play now?" he turned to his father, this time waiting for his nod before charging off into the circle of wagons looking for other children.

"You did real good keepin' an eye on that little fella," Mrs. Hampton sidled up to Daliah with a dish rag and began drying dishes as Daliah washed. "I think he's going to need someone looking out for him, with his father busy all the time."

"I'm happy to help in any way I can," Daliah agreed, knowing that Mrs. Hampton had already decided to take the boy under her wing.

"Good, between us, we should be able to keep him close about. I wouldn't like to see him wander off and get lost or something."

"How many miles did we make today?" Mr. Hampton asked Spencer, who was now drinking coffee by the fire, enjoying a leftover piece of pie as he listened to the night sounds around him.

"About fifteen, which isn't bad. We may get a few twenty-mile days in if the weather stays good.

The stock is fresh and the air is cool."

"Twenty miles a day," Mr. Hampton mused. "That'd be a nice start."

"It's good to be out and moving again. It takes a lot to get a train like this going and once it starts, the best thing is to get settled into the daily routine and keep marching." Spencer said. "Trust me, though. You'll be sick of it soon enough."

"Probably true," Mr. Hampton agreed, then jumped to his feet as his wife cried out in pain.

"Olive, what's wrong?" he asked, hurrying toward her as Daliah wrapped a towel around his wife's hand.

"Oh, how careless of me," Mrs. Hampton cried. "One day on the trail and I cut my hand something terrible." She peeled the towel away to peek at the pool of blood in her palm, but Daliah pressed it tight again.

"You take a seat now, Mrs. Hampton. You need to keep pressure on this for a bit. Hold it tight while I'll mix up some honey salve for it."

Daliah hurried to the back of the wagon while Mr. Hampton helped his wife take a seat on a crate, patting her back soothingly.

A few minutes later, Daliah smeared a mixture

of honey, salt, and fat onto the cut and bandaged it up tight. "Don't you worry about a thing, Mrs. Hampton. I'll take care of the cooking and packing. You look after that hand and see that it heals up properly."

Spencer watched the interaction between the two women. Miss Owens seemed a capable sort. They needed women like that on a long trail. Needed women like that in the town they were going to. He only hoped she didn't get in his way as they pushed toward Texas. Most of the people on the train were young families or single men with a few older folks in the mix. It was a small troupe, but if they worked together, getting to the tiny, no-name town his brother had urged him to get to in Texas shouldn't take long.

For a moment, he wondered where the Hamptons and the pretty Miss Owens would settle once they got to Texas. He knew some folks had kin in different locations and that they would break off heading to various areas at the end of the line. Shaking his head, he cast the thoughts away. He didn't need any woman interfering in his life.

Chapter 5

"Daliah, I feel terrible for all the extra work you have to do," Mrs. Hampton said the next morning as they organized to leave. You should let me do something," she said, shaking her head.

"You don't need to do a thing," Daliah said, smiling at the older woman. "If it weren't for you, just think where I'd be right now. This is my way of paying you back."

Mrs. Hampton smiled, nodding her acceptance. Daliah had certainly suffered enough loss in her life for someone so young and then to have insult added to injury at the bank. Olive had been furious when her boarder, a young woman alone in the world, had been dismissed.

The older woman climbed into the wagon, adjusting the softer materials and checking that everything was where it belonged with her good hand while Orville and Daliah finished putting out the fire and hitching the team. It was exciting to be starting a new adventure and even if they didn't like Texas, they could say they tried. It had been a tearful goodbye with her three sons and their families, but rumors had it that the railroad would be connecting to Texas shortly, anyway. Then they could journey back to visit family or go East to see the sights whenever they wanted.

The sound of a galloping horse made Mrs. Hampton peer out the back of the wagon and smile as Mr. Gaines rode by with his little boy. Those two young men needed a woman to look after them, and if she had her way, they would have one before this trek was over.

**

Spencer cantered past the last wagon, noting that the camp was squared away and the team hitched. He tipped his hat as he rode by but didn't say anything. He needed to get the lead wagons rolling or they wouldn't make any time at all throughout the day.

In front of him, his sleepy son squirmed and yawned. It was hard on the boy traveling this way. On his last few treks, Chad had stayed with family, but this time was different. This time when he reached Texas, they would settle and stay there.

Spencer would use his pay and what he had saved to start a new life and put the past behind him. He had been surprised when the whole idea of heading to Texas had taken off with so many, and what he was making helping to lead the train would go a long way toward a new life.

"I'm hungry, Pa," Chad said softly.

"You just ate," Spencer replied as he hurried to get the train on the move. His partner Ben was still helping another family get set to roll, and Spencer needed to take the lead today.

"I'll see if I can get you something in a bit," Spencer said. "I've got some jerky in my pack you can chew for now."

Chad wrinkled his nose at the thought of jerky but didn't say anything. Instead, he leaned back into his father and closed his eyes against the gray light of a new day.

"Pa, I'm still hungry," Chad whined a half-hour later as the wagons stretched out in a slow-moving line past his stationary horse toward the horizon. "You said you'd get me something to eat."

The Hampton wagon was coming up along his flank now as the boy grumbled and Mrs. Hampton waved the pair over.

"Give that boy to me, Mr. Gaines," the older woman called, waving him toward the wagon. "I've got a couple of biscuits here he can have, and I don't see any reason he should be stuck in the saddle with you all day. Heaven knows I'm no use for anything else, but he can ride along with Orville and me for a bit."

"If you're sure you don't mind," Spencer said, trying to keep the relief out of his voice as he sidled up to the wagon and let Chad climb in behind the older couple. At the back of the wagon, the pretty young woman tipped her head from under her oversized hat and smiled as she walked along the edge of the trail, and Spencer scowled at the impact her lovely dark eyes had on him.

"We don't mind. Do we, Orville?" Mrs. Hampton said. "It'll make me feel useful while my hand heals. You come on back at noon again, and we'll fix you both up with a meal."

Spencer nodded, looking his son in the eye as he turned to go. "You be good, and I'll see you later," he said, but Chad just grinned around the biscuit he was busy devouring.

Daliah watched Mr. Gaines ride away. She couldn't fathom what the wagon master could have been thinking, bringing his young son along this way. Perhaps if the man were driving his wagon instead of hiring someone else to move it or had relatives to help watch the boy, it would have made sense, but to expect a growing boy to ride all day like that was hard. Children needed room to stretch out and explore.

There were other children in the train, of course, and Daliah hoped that in time Chad would be able to make friends or perhaps even travel with some of the families, but for now, with most people still virtual strangers, she supposed they would have to do their best.

Morning was barely a suggestion of day at the moment, and the young woman couldn't help but wonder what the day would hold. She had so many mixed emotions about the trip and her future. She had agreed to come to give herself a new start but also to help the Hamptons. They were no longer young, and from all, she had heard the trip to Texas was difficult. Perhaps one day, the dream of rail travel would be realized everywhere, but for now, if you were moving, this was the only way to go.

In a way, the fact that Mrs. Hampton had cut her hand was a blessing because she had no choice but to let Daliah do more of the work that she should be doing, anyway. Daliah had always enjoyed helping others, and it wasn't hard when they were people you loved. Mr. and Mrs. Hampton were almost like family to Daliah. They were the only people she had on this earth who cared for her.

Placing one foot in front of the other, Daliah breathed deeply of the early morning air setting her eyes toward the horizon and the new day.

Everything was fresh and she longed to know where the trail would ultimately lead.

Chapter 6

"Daliah, Billy has skinned his knuckles again," a petite woman called, walking back toward the Hampton wagon with a boy of about six in tow. "Do you have any more of that salve?"

"Of course, Aida. I'll get it now," Daliah smiled, keeping pace with the wagon then grabbing the tail gate to pull herself up. Several of the women in the train, on hearing of Daliah's salve, had asked for her help, and she was glad she could give it. Children always seemed to be doing something.

They had been on the trail for nearly three weeks now, and although Mrs. Hampton's hand was healed, Daliah still tried to keep the other woman from doing too much. Her mother had taught her to make the honey salve, and it seemed to work wonders on cuts, scrapes, and abrasions.

"Here you are," Daliah called, handing the small jar out of the wagon to Aida Smith.

"You're such a help," Aida said, stopping and smearing some of the yellow salve on her son's hand. "You go on now, Billy," she said, falling into step with Daliah as she climbed from the wagon.

"How's the trail treating you?" Daliah asked as they walked along at the edge of the trail. "Is your daughter feeling better?"

"Beth is so much better," Aida said, "that elixir you made for her has knocked that cough right out. She's taking a nap in the wagon now, thank goodness," the tiny woman added.

Daliah felt like an Amazon from the story books walking next to her petite neighbor. Though not overly tall, Aida made her feel huge. She doubted that the woman was much over four foot nine, but she was so full of energy. She had come to Missouri to marry a man she had never met and take on a life as a mother for Billy. Now she had her own little girl, and she and her husband Terry planned on starting a brand new life in Texas.

"What do you think it will be like in Texas?" Daliah asked.

"I think it will be wild," Aida said, grinning. "I hear that in the spring, the hills are covered in blue bonnets as far as the eye can see. I'm looking forward to having a farm and a few animals," she finished.

Daliah smiled. "That sounds lovely. I heard that most of it is desert with cactus and sand everywhere."

"I think that's further south," Aida said, shaking her head as the sound of boys arguing caught her ear. "Where will you stop?" the other woman asked.

Daliah shook her head. She didn't know the exact plans that the Hamptons had made. Would they travel further south into the desert or stay in the hill country? "I'm not sure," she confessed. "I plan on sticking with the Hamptons as long as they'll have me," she said, dropping her eyes as a sense of loneliness enveloped her.

"They're lucky to have you," Aida said, squeezing Daliah's arm as a brawl broke out somewhere along the line. "I have to go before Trey gets in over his head," she said with a laugh, lifting her skirts and trotting toward where her son was yelling at Chad.

Daliah adjusted the old hat on her head and watched as Aida broke up the two boys sending Chad back toward her with a flea in his ear. The boy's manner left a great deal to be desired, and he was always trying to take things from the other children.

For a moment, Daliah wondered if she would ever have children to love. She was already twenty and had never had a beau. She pondered what made a happy marriage like the one the Hamptons had, but even as she thought it, she pushed the notion aside. She would be content to look after the Hamptons and help them settle into their new lives. She had already said goodbye to so many loved ones that part of her just wanted to hide away from everyone she could care for.

The sound of a galloping horse caught her attention and Daliah looked up to see Mr. Gaines riding toward her. The man leaned low in the saddle as he approached his son, dipping sideways to scoop the boy onto the fast-moving horse.

Daliah covered her heart with her hands as her feet froze to the spot. What if Mr. Gaines had missed and Chad had been injured?

"Afternoon," Mr. Gaines said, slowing his horse as he approached, then scowled as he took in Daliah's pale appearance. "You feeling all right, Miss Owens?"

"Yes, yes," Daliah stammered, pulling herself back together. "I'm afraid your performance just now rather startled me, is all."

"I'm sorry, I didn't mean to frighten you. I've been picking Chad up like that for a long time. We used to have a small cattle ranch, you see, and we made a game of it."

Daliah smiled, feeling relieved but still wondering if it was wise to do such things. It wasn't her business, though, so she kept quiet. Although Chad was often with her or Mrs. Hampton, he wasn't her responsibility.

"I rode back to let everyone know that we'll be stopping for the night on the far side of that ridge. There's plenty of water and a good place to rest for a couple of days."

"That sounds wonderful," Daliah agreed. "Perhaps we can catch up on a few things that need attention while the stock gets a chance to rest."

"That's the plan," Spencer said smiling. He was surprised that the young woman's first thoughts were of the work and maintenance that needed doing and not the idea of a much-needed rest. Perhaps there was more to this girl than he had first realized. Despite himself, Spencer had noticed her helping others around the camp or working with Mrs. Hampton. He'd tried to stop and share a meal with most of the families in the wagon train, but he found himself drawn back to the last wagon on the line again and again.

"Will you be joining us for dinner tonight?" Daliah asked as if reading his thoughts.

"I hope so," Chad piped up. "I like the cookin' here best," he finished.

Daliah smiled. "Mrs. Hampton is a very good cook," she admitted. "I think the plan is for a big pot of beans and sour dough biscuits tonight. She's asked me to make a bit of cinnamon bread as well if I can."

"Can ya?" Chad asked, his bright eyes full of

hope.

"I'll do my best," Daliah chuckled. "You're both welcome as always."

Spencer looked down at the young woman. She couldn't be more than twenty, but she seemed older for her years. Mr. Hampton had told him a bit of her story, and he understood what it felt like to be alone in the world. It was one of the reasons he had agreed to join his brother in Texas. Would it be such a bad thing to consider a woman in his life? Wouldn't it be better to have someone like Daliah to look after Chad?

Shaking the thoughts from his head Spencer nodded once. "We'll be back around for supper," he said, tipping his hat, then turning his mount and trotting back toward the leads.

Daliah watched the trail boss trot away down the line. He was tall and lean and sat straight in the saddle. He was a nice-looking man, and she hoped that God would bless him and help him raise that boy. She had done her best so far to keep young Chad out of trouble. Now, if everyone could keep up with that, they might get to Texas unscathed.

***

Supper came late that night as one of the wagons had trouble with a wheel pin that day and had slowed progress, but when they had all rolled down over the slight rise into a valley filled with fresh grass and a slow-moving river, the collected group had issued a sigh of delight.

Two days of cleaning clothes, washing dishes, and resting the stock would go a long way to boosting morale among the trail weary troupe.

"Mr. Gaines," Mrs. Hampton called as the man rode up, dropping his son to the ground. "Daliah said you'd be by for supper, and we've fixed up a nice dish."

"Sit and rest a spell," Mr. Hampton called, encouraging the man and boy to join them.

"Somethin' smells good," Chad said, slipping onto an old log next to Orville.

"I'm sure you're hungry," Mrs. Hampton said, handing the boy a plate full of beans and a hot buttered biscuit, then gave another to his father.

"Thank you," Spencer said, turning to look at Miss Owens, who had just placed something else on the grid over the fire.

"Aren't you eating?" he asked without thinking.

"I'm just getting this started first," Daliah replied. "We all want dessert, don't we?"

Chapter 7

Spencer watched the young woman move around the campfire, talking quietly to Mrs. Hampton as she placed the tray of something over the fire.

Only a blind man wouldn't recognize that she was a pretty girl with a rather inviting shape. Not for the first time he wondered about her story. Mr. Hampton had told him when he signed on to the drive that she'd lost both of her parents on the way to Missouri and then her brother more recently. He wondered why she hadn't returned east to other family members.

Of course, he had also heard from a few other towns' folk that she had been dismissed from her job at the bank for stealing, and he questioned her motives for coming along with the Hamptons. Could she be hoping to gain something from the older couple?

Daliah looked up and smiled, noting the pensive look in Mr. Gaines' eyes. Evidently, he had been studying her, and she wondered if she had done something that he didn't approve of. She had mixed up a tray of cinnamon bread using the sourdough starter earlier that afternoon, and now it was ready to cook in the small covered tray she had settled over the coals.

Spencer watched Daliah dazzled by her kind smile as she fiddled with whatever it was she was cooking, then picked up a plate and served her supper. She was pretty. She seemed so kind. It just didn't make sense that she might have done something wrong. Still here, she was on the trail and not long unemployed. He would keep an eye on things as they traveled to see what kind of woman she really was.

"Daliah makes the best cinnamon bread," Mrs. Hampton said from her perch on a cracker barrel. "Her mother must have been a whiz in the kitchen. I'm glad she agreed to make some for us today since we'll be on the road again before you know it. How many loaves, dear?" she asked, looking to Daliah, who took the crate next to her.

"I'm making four," Daliah said. "I tried not to be heavy-handed with the supplies, though," she added, "but I did want to have some for the week as well."

Chad lifted his nose toward the fire, his eyes gleaming in the soft light. "Sure smells good," he said. "Can I have some?"

"Of course, you can have some," Mrs. Hampton said. "What's the fun of making it if we can't share?"

"I'd rather not share," Chad admitted.

"If we all thought like that," Daliah said, "then you wouldn't be here, and I wouldn't give you any of my bread."

The boy studied her for a moment, then nodded, his unruly blonde hair falling in his eyes. "I'd still rather have it all to myself," he confessed, "but I guess it makes sense."

The adults chuckled. It was never easy learning to share and help others. Too often, people only thought of their own needs in this world, but if we try hard and put our faith in God, we could be much more than we ever dreamed of.

"Chad, behave yourself," Spencer chided gently. "We're guests at this fire."

"More like friends," Orville said, slapping Spencer on the back. "You've done a good job helping us out, and we like to repay the favor."

Spencer grinned. It did feel like the Hamptons were more like friends than just people he was working for. On the other hand, it felt odd after so many years to feel as if he was welcome somewhere again.

"Where will you be settling when you get to

Texas, anyway?" Orville asked, wiping his plate clean with an extra biscuit.

"My brother has a place at the lower end of the hill country," Spencer said. "He's started a little cattle outfit, and there's good water and feed. A few other folks are trying to make a go of it farming. Dan reckons there will be a proper town there before long. There's a sort of tent town already."

"Now, doesn't that sound nice," Mr. Hampton said. "Maybe we'll trail along there with you if they need more folks. I'm sure if folks are thinking of settling, it will be needing a good many people and skills."

"That's what my brother keeps saying," Spencer said, looking up as Daliah finished her meal and began collecting plates.

"What will you do there?" the young woman asked.

"Probably raise cattle with my brother," Spencer replied. "I used to have cows a while back."

"And I'm gonna have my own pony and ride all over the place shooting prairie dogs and ropin' cows," Chad added, making everyone smile.

Spencer laughed, ruffling his son's hair. "Well, I think we can manage the pony," he said. "As for the rest, we might have to wait a spell on that."

"Ah Pa," Chad grumbled, pushing his father's

hand away. "I'll be big by the time we get to Texas."

Everyone laughed at the boy's misconception, but he ignored them, rising and walking to the fire as he tried to peer into the pan of bread.

"You be careful," Spencer said as the boy teetered on his tiptoes. Everyone gasped as Chad turned, the toe of his boot catching on a rock as he began to fall.

Spencer sprang to his feet but wasn't fast enough as his son began to fall. In an instant, a strong arm reached out, snatching the boy back from the brink of danger as Daliah grabbed him.

"That is very dangerous," Daliah chided. "You could have been badly hurt. Fire is nothing to play with."

Chad looked up at her as she settled him on the ground once more. "I ain't hurt," he grumbled. "I was just lookin' at the bread."

"Next time, don't look so close," his father said, taking his hand and leading him back to the log. "You don't need to be messing about with fire and such."

"I didn't do nothin' Pa," Chad grumbled.

"Just leave the cooking to the woman, son," Spencer said. "You'll be glad you did."

Everyone around the fire chuckled, easing the tension of a moment ago as they relaxed once

DANNI ROAN

more.

Spencer felt his heart settling back into a steady rhythm. He was grateful that the young woman had been in the right place at the right moment to save his son from certain injury. Would a woman who had stolen from a bank be willing to put herself in danger for a stranger's son? He didn't know. He was just thankful that Chad was unharmed.

48

Chapter 8

Spencer saddled his horse the next day, shoving his rifle into the scabbard as he scanned the surrounding plains. He and a few of the other men were headed out to do some hunting, and if all went well, they would have a deer or at least a few rabbits to share for supper.

"Do I have to stay with that old lady today?" Chad whined. "Why can't I come with you?"

"You're too young for hunting," Spencer said, "besides, I thought you liked Mrs. Hampton."

"I like her food pretty good, so I guess she's all right."

"You ate three pieces of that bread last night," Spencer chuckled. "I think you must like the food at that wagon."

Chad shrugged. "I'll go play with the other kids," he said. "I hope you bring back something good."

Spencer shook his head as the scamp raced off to play with his friends. The camp was alive with the bustle of industry as women gathered clothing and headed to the river to wash while men tended stock, checked gear, and mended rigs.

Swinging into the saddle, he turned toward the prairie and started looking for a deer sign. He was surprised at how well things had been going so far for the train. They had about another month of travel before they would go their separate ways, and he hoped that things continued well.

Even Chad had been staying out of trouble for the most part, and Spencer knew it was primarily due to the watchful eye of Mrs. Hampton and Miss Owens.

The morning warmed as Spencer rode farther afield, scouting and watching for any indication of deer. Fresh meat would go a long way with a small train like this, and he hoped he would have good luck.

About mid-morning, he came on a small game trail and eased his rifle from its scabbard.

***

"Chad, you get away from the edge of the water now," Mrs. Hampton called, waving at the young boy who was standing on the edge of the river. In a quieter spot, some of the other children were splashing under the watchful eye of their mothers, but here where they were doing, wash the water was faster, and she didn't want him to fall in.

"I ain't doing nothin' wrong," the boy sassed. "I'm just looking for fish," he finished.

Mrs. Hampton turned the garment in her hand, slapping it onto the wide rock beside her as she scrubbed the dirt and trail dust from it only to scream when a loud splash made her turn her head.

Chad had stepped too close to the edge and had toppled into the river.

"Help, help!" Mrs. Hampton cried, but before she had finished her call for help, Daliah had plunged into the river, fully dressed, grasping the boy by the britches and hauling him to shore.

"I think Mrs. Hampton told you not to get too close," Daliah spluttered as she placed the boy on dry land then hauled herself and her sodden skirts from the cold water. "I had not planned on doing my wash with me in it," she finished giving the boy a stern look.

Chad climbed to his feet, shaking the water from his hair. "I would have been all right," he insisted.

"So you can swim?" Daliah said, placing her hands on her hips.

"Well, not proper yet," Chad admitted, "but I'll learn."

Daliah turned to look at Mrs. Hampton, who was

getting herself back under control. "I'll take him to the lead wagon and see if there are clean clothes there for him," she said quietly, wringing out her skirt disgustedly.

It was bad enough she had burnt her hand the night before, keeping the boy from falling into the fire. Now she was soaked from head to toe and would have to find clean clothes for both of them.

"Chad, you do realize that when you don't listen to the adults here, you are putting yourself in danger, don't you?" Daliah said, as together, they trudged back to the wagon.

"Well, my pa can do anything, so why can't I?" Chad bristled.

"Because you are only a boy," Daliah said gently. "You have to grow into a man before you can do all of the things your Pa does."

Chad looked up at Daliah seriously. He was cold and wet and falling in the river had scared him more than he was willing to admit. However, he was glad Daliah had been there to help him and perhaps he should listen to her a little more. Well, as long as she didn't ruin his fun.

He and his pa had been just fine before they took off on this wagon train, and they would be just fine when all the other people around now had gone away. No one stayed long. They never stayed anywhere long. It was just him and his Pa that was all that mattered.

Daliah looked down at the boy who trudged along the path beside her. He didn't make friends easily, often fighting and arguing or taking the other children's things. He didn't listen well or follow instructions either, for that matter. Perhaps in time, he would trust her enough to know she was trying to look out for him.

They had just made the break to the wagons when a horse approached and Mr. Gaines pulled up in front of them, the carcass of a deer draped across his saddle bows.

"What happened to you?" he asked, looking at the half-drowned rats before him.

"I fell in," Chad said, grinning, "and Daliah pulled me out."

Spencer looked at the young woman, his eyes growing wide. "Thank you," he said, grateful that for the second time in as many days, she had kept his son from harm.

"Anyone would have done the same," Daliah said. "I'm glad that I was near."

Spencer ran a hand behind his neck and cringed. Was the woman criticizing him for being gone? They had needed fresh meat, and he had delivered.

"Daliah, you go get yourself into something dry," Mrs. Hampton said, walking over and draping a blanket over Chad's shoulders. "You hand down that deer, and me and Orville will get it butchered while you get this boy changed," she finished giving Mr. Gaines a curt nod.

Spencer nodded. He would be glad when this trial ended, and he could start building a proper home for his son.

An hour later, with the help of some of the other women and her husband, Mrs. Hampton had a roast turning on a spit as the savory smell of fresh venison roasting over an open fire filled the area as folks gathered around preparing special dishes to share.

A festive atmosphere seemed to spring to life with the fresh meat, and soon everyone was pulling together to finish chores before sharing a meal.

"What can I help with?" Daliah asked, returning to the fire and hanging her wet dress nearby.

"I think Mr. Woolsey was complaining about his lumbago," Mr. Hampton said. "Why don't you go along and see about him while I get supper ready tonight. Your ointment might help him."

Daliah nodded, returning to the wagon for the few items she had brought with her. Her mother had been gifted with home remedies, and she had learned how to use them to good effect by helping her mother on the trip west.

Several of the women in the wagon train had already asked her for headache powders or ointment to soothe scraped or chapped hands.

Daliah was glad that she could do something to make others more comfortable. She only wished she didn't have the cloud of doubt hanging over her head after the unpleasantness at the bank.

There were still those who felt that if she hadn't done anything wrong, she wouldn't have been dismissed. One man, traveling without his family, had even gone so far as to ask her where she'd hidden the extra money.

By the time Daliah had helped Mr. Woolsey rub the ointment on his aching shoulder and wrapped it in warm flannel, dinner was ready and she returned to the fire amidst the laughter and cheerful babble of the rest of the wagon train.

Stepping up to the fire, Daliah automatically began serving others, but when Mr. Hampton told her to fix her plate and take a seat, she did as she was asked. Every day Daliah thanked the good Lord for the Hamptons. She didn't know what would have become of her without them.

"You can sit with me," Chad said, patting the log next to him as he scooted closer to his father.

"Thank you," Daliah said. It was jarring how sometimes the boy had such pleasant manners, and other times he seemed to run like a wild animal completely un-tethered.

"Is something wrong with old Mr. Woolsey?" Spencer asked, scooping up a fork full of potatoes and crisp roast meat.

"Just his lumbago," Daliah said. "Nothing to worry about if he keeps it warm tonight. He should be right as rain tomorrow."

Spencer looked up out of habit, gazing at the stars to judge the weather for the next day. He hoped there wouldn't be any rain the next day.

"What are you looking for?" Daliah asked, gazing up at the sparkle of stars above.

"Checkin' the weather," Spencer said roughly. "I'm hoping we won't end up with too much rain. The prairie gets muddy and slows everything down."

"Have you been across this way before?" Daliah asked.

"A time or two," Spencer admitted. "My brother has a small cattle spread down in Texas and we stopped there a couple of years ago. It was pretty rough at the time, though, and with Chad to think of, I moved on."

"But you're going back now?" Daliah was curious as to the man's intentions. He was quiet, bossy, and taciturn, but she still felt something in him that was familiar. A sense of loneliness and longing that, if she were honest, echoed in her soul.

"Seems a few of the ranches in the area are hoping to get a town started," Spencer said. "That's why we're all headed that way instead of to Oregon. There's been talk the past couple of years about bringing a railroad to Texas, and when that happens, men like my brother won't have to push their herds up the Chisholm Trail to sell."

"That sounds difficult," Daliah agreed, not even noticing when Chad reached up and stole her cornbread. "Do they lose many cows that way?"

"A few," Spencer said. "Longhorns move pretty good and can feed well on the drive, but there are still rustlers, stampedes, and swollen rivers to deal with."

Daliah laid her hand over her heart. "It sounds like a dangerous job," she said.

Spencer shrugged broad shoulders, pulling the fabric of his shirt tight. "Can be, but if you get a good price for your herd, it's worth it, and in a year or two, you'll have another bunch of cows to sell again."

"Is your brother married," Daliah asked, not sure where the question had sprung from.

"No, he's on his own. He hasn't ever been married, but being the youngest, he has time if he wants it." He grinned then, surprising Daliah, who noted how his face lit up when he smiled. "Problem is there ain't hardly any young eligible women thereabouts."

Daliah smiled. "Perhaps as the town grows, there will be more people and a better opportunity for your brother to find someone suitable," she said, offering her own smile.

They talked a few minutes longer before Daliah heard someone call out in pain and ran to help. Another careless burn was only a minor distraction on the trail.

Chapter 9

The following day Daliah woke feeling happy to be back on the trail after her discussion with Mr. Gaines the night before. She felt that surely in a brand new town, she could make a fresh start for herself. She wondered if there were any jobs she might do or perhaps she could start a business of her own.

The idea of her own place, her own job, and being her own boss appealed to her. She was good with simple remedies and helping those with minor injuries or illnesses. Perhaps she could sell some of her salves or ointments.

As the morning rolled into afternoon, her mind was so full of thoughts of the future that she walked right past the Hampton's wagon and on to the next.

"Miss Owens?" a warm, rich voice washed over her, making her stop and look up to see Mr. Gaines and Chad.

"Oh, good morning," Daliah said, tipping her hat up, so she could see the man.

"Can I come eat with you?" Chad asked, squirming out of his father's grasp and dropping to the ground. "I'm hungry."

"You are always welcome at our fire," Daliah said with a laugh.

"See, Pa, I told you that she wouldn't care. The lady with the big hat always likes it when I come for lunch."

Daliah couldn't help but laugh. The boy was precocious, and she did think he needed a lesson in manners, but he still made her smile. "Will you be joining us, Mr. Gaines?"

"I might be back," Spencer said, leaning on his saddle horn and scanning their surroundings with a keen eye.

"I'll save you something Pa," Chad said, taking Daliah's hand and dragging her toward her wagon where Mr. Hampton was already setting up the camp stove.

Spencer sat up straight, turning his horse back along the line to see that everyone had heard the word for noonin'. Even at their pace, horses and oxen needed a rest and a chance to feed. It had been a clean run so far, but anything could happen when you weren't looking."

Casting a glance back over his shoulder, he watched the pert young woman walking along next to his son. Chad deserved a mother, but there was no room in his heart for that. When he'd lost his wife, he'd given up on all of that nonsense. He was sure he would manage just fine on his own, and as the boy got older, it would only get easier.

Something nagged at the back of Spencer's mind trying to force him to recognize the lie, but he pushed it away. At least in Texas, his son would have family. He could grow strong and tall in the wide-open spaces of the Lone Star State, learning to work cattle and build something that would eventually be his.

At the far side of the line, Spencer saw a horse step in a hole and he kicked his mount forward toward the team, hoping a broken leg wouldn't mean that they had to put the animal down.

"Mr. Gaines," a young man in a straw hat called, holding tight to the horse's reins. "I think his foot is stuck."

Spencer jumped from the saddle, soothing the spooked horse and helping the boy hold him steady while they checked the leg. Squeezing his fingers into a crevice, he wiggled a rock loose and the horse pulled its hoof free.

Holding his breath Spencer went over the horse's leg, finding a tender fetlock but no serious harm.

"I'll get some liniment for this leg," Spencer said,

striding back to his horse. You keep him easy and let him graze. Hopefully, he'll be fine by the time we take off again."

"Yes, sir," the man said, stroking the big horse's nose.

"Miss Owens, do you have anything for a bruised leg?" Spencer asked, jumping from his saddle as his horse skidded to a stop.

"Of course," Daliah said, handing Chad a plate and heading for the wagon. "Did you hurt yourself?"

"Not me," Spencer said. "One of the Matthews' horses."

"Oh, I don't know that it has ever been used on a horse before," Daliah said. "Don't overdo it," she added, starting to hand him the pot. Pulling it back, she looked at the man's unhappy face. "I think I'd better do it," she finally said. "Take me to this horse,"

"You don't need to trouble yourself," Spencer said. "Just give me the pot."

"No," Daliah said, feeling mildly embarrassed. "I'm afraid this is all I have and I can't have it being wasted," Daliah insisted.

"Fine," Spencer growled, grabbing his horse's reins. "Climb up."

"I'll walk," Daliah said.

"We don't have time," Spencer said, grabbing her around the waist and swinging her up onto the horse as her breath left her lungs.

"Mr. Gaines," Daliah protested, clutching the saddle horn where she sat across the saddle swells.

Spencer swung up behind the young woman threading his arms around her and taking the reins as he trotted toward the other wagon. He couldn't help but smile at the little squeal of fright the woman gave. She should have just given the stuff to him.

Five minutes later, Spencer admitted that he had been wrong. He would have used far more of the balm than Miss Owens had and based on how the horse kept stomping its foot, the stuff was plenty powerful enough.

"If you'll excuse me," Daliah said, screwing the top back on the jar. "I need to go wash my hands." Then, before the man could react, she was striding through the camp toward her wagon, her head held high in irritation.

Climbing into the wagon quickly and putting her jar away, Daliah tried to settle her breathing. Mr. Gaines was a complex man, and she didn't want to fight with him, but she also could see a need in him that she couldn't quite place. It was as if some force warred within him that she couldn't understand, and his treatment of her today was only a symptom of the disease as a whole.

The man loved his son but couldn't seem to take the time to sort out the boy's behavior. He was hard working and took great care to provide for those who rode with him, but he didn't get close to anyone.

She wondered if he had been a very different man before he had lost his wife. Perhaps he had been cheerful and fun-loving or deeply caring and full of hope for a bright future.

Bowing her head Daliah said a prayer for Mr. Gaines and Chad, determining in her heart to keep a closer watch on the boy. Someone needed to help Mr. Gaines with the child, and she would do all she could to keep him safe and out of trouble.

Stepping back out of the wagon a few minutes later, Daliah hurried to the fire where Chad was chatting at Mrs. Hampton.

"We're just warming up the stew I made last night," Mrs. Hampton said, "but maybe Daliah will make us some biscuits to go with it," she added, smiling at the young woman as she approached.

"I'd be glad to," Daliah agreed, tying her apron around her middle.

"Can we have honey on 'em?" Chad asked.

"How about jam instead?" Daliah asked. She wanted to keep some of the honey for her cough medicine and other healing items she mixed up when needed. Thinking of it made her miss her mother keenly today. Her mother had taught her so much over the years and had tried to instill a deep sense of kindness and giving in Daliah.

"Why do you look sad?" Chad asked, peering up into her face. Children could be so discerning at times.

"I was thinking of my mother," Daliah admitted with a soft smile.

"I don't hardly remember my ma," Chad said, "but I got a blanket she made me, and Pa says it's special 'cause she made it just for me."

Daliah's heart warmed to the boy, and she smiled. "I'm sure your mother loved you very much," she said.

The boy shrugged, tossing a stick into the small fire. "What happened to your ma?" he asked.

"My mother and father died of a fever," Daliah said, checking the biscuits she had cooking on the fire.

"I'm glad I got my Pa," Chad said. "He said we're movin' to live with my uncle Dan, and I can have my own pony," he finished with an excited smile.

"I'm sure you'll be a great help to your father in your new home," Daliah said, grinning.

Again the boy shrugged. "Is it time to eat yet?"

"In a few minutes," Mrs. Hampton called. "You go fetch your father and then we'll eat."

The boy took off shouting for his father as he raced down the line of wagons, making Daliah smile.

"That boy needs a woman to love him," Mrs. Hampton said. "I can see he and his pa have been on their own too long," she continued shaking her wooden spoon for emphasis. "I think I'd best pray Mr. Gaines up a wife."

Daliah gaped at the older woman wondering how she could say such a thing. She was sure that if Mr. Gaines were interested in a wife, he would find one. Still, she wondered if he felt as alone in the world as she did sometimes. If not for her faith and the ability to talk to God, or his blessing of Mr. and Mrs. Hampton, Daliah would indeed be on her alone. Perhaps it wouldn't be wrong to pray that Mr. Gaines found someone to fill that all too familiar hole in his heart.

Chapter 10

"Oh, Daliah, please come quick!" Alice Scripts cried as she hurried around the wagon in the pre-dawn light. "Trey's spilled boiling water all down his side, and I don't know what to do," the woman sniffled. "Hurry!"

Grabbing up a wad of towels, Daliah dashed after the portly woman hefting the bucket of water from a peg on the side of the prairie schooner.

Making the turn, she took in the scene where a boy of perhaps fourteen struggled to get his shirt off as tears poured from his eyes.

"Mama, help!" the boy pleaded, shocked when Daliah poured the icy water over the steaming section of cloth, before grabbing the shirt and shredding it in strong hands.

"Don't worry, Trey," Daliah said, her kind voice soft and assuring, "everything will be all right."

The young man looked toward his mother, fear and doubt shimmering in his eyes, even as his

DANNI ROAN

mother nodded.

"Mrs. Script, will you please go to Mrs. Hampton," Daliah said. "Tell her I need my burn cream." Behind her, Daliah could hear the woman hurry away. "What happened, Trey?" she asked as she grabbed the wet shirt and gently pushed it against the red and white mottled welts running under the boy's armpit and down his side.

"Can you fix it?" he asked, his voice shaking with fear and doubt. "Ma needs my help to travel. If I can't use my arm..." his voice faded as he swallowed hard.

"I'll do everything I can," Daliah said, smiling her confidence. "I've seen much worse, and those people healed up just fine, but you'll have to do exactly what I say. It won't be easy." Her bright eyes bore into his and the boy nodded, pushing aside his fear and focusing on her words.

Mrs. Script arrived holding a clay jar in her hand. "Is this what you need?" she said, her voice breaking as she saw the terrible welts and blisters on her son's body.

"That's perfect," Daliah said, taking the jar. "Now, if you'll start brewing a pot of very strong tea."

Mrs. Script looked at Daliah, oddly confused about the request.

"Just do it," Daliah said firmly. "I'll explain later," she finished turning and carefully smearing the cold, cream-like substance on Trey's injury. "This will hurt in a minute," she said, taking the boy's eyes with hers. "You focus on me, and we'll get through it together."

***

Spencer reined his horse to a stop at the back of the Script wagon watching as Daliah tended to young Trey. He'd heard the young man cry out earlier and hurried to see what was wrong, but Daliah was already there. It seemed that the longer they traveled, the more people depended on her for help with injuries, illness, or even stock issues. The young woman in the floppy hat had a healing hand and soft presence that put others at ease.

The lean trail boss couldn't help but think of how she had helped look after his son keeping him out of trouble more often than not and protecting Chad from himself.

Scowling, he thought of Chad's newest scrape with old Mr. Franco the night before. It had been all he could do to keep the older man from whipping the boy with his fiddle bow when Chad had grabbed the man's elegant old fiddle and plucked the strings.

No matter how he looked at it, Spencer knew he needed help with his son, but he would worry about that once they got safely to Texas.

He watched a while longer as Daliah held tight to Trey's hands while whatever was in the cream she had smeared on his burns began to work, and the boy choked on his tears, fighting the pain.

"Just look at me, Trey," Daliah crooned. "Soon, we'll be in Texas, and you'll be in the cold streams swimming with your friends or riding out into the snow of the coldest winter. Why I've heard that Texas has springs as blue as the sky that trickle, cold as an ice puddle, even in June."

Spencer could see that the woman's knuckles were white as she gripped the boy's hands, keeping him perfectly still even as he jerked and bucked against the pain.

"I know it burns right now," Daliah continued but think of the snow in winter, the cold springs of summer, and all the things you'll do when you join your Pa at your new home."

Slowly Trey began to relax as a cool breeze whispered across the prairie, ruffling his hair and cooling the grease smeared on his injury.

Daliah eased her grip on the boy as the cool air took some of the sting from the herbs in the cream she had put on the burn. She knew from experience how much the ointment stung in the beginning, but in the end, it stole the lasting pain away.

"That's better now, isn't it?" She said with a smile laying his hands on his knees and resting one of hers over them. "You have to keep your arm from chafing against that burn," she said. "If your shirt sticks to it or your arm rubs it, you could end up with an infection. Do you understand?"

"Yes, ma'am," Trey said, his breathing slowing to normal again as the searing pain subsided.

"Here's your tea," Mrs. Scripts said, walking toward Daliah with a mug.

Daliah shook her head. "Put it in a pan and let it cool," she said, lifting Trey's arms up and nodding for him to keep them there. "You'll need to make compresses of it for the next few days."

Mrs. Script looked between Daliah and her son, her face pale. Walking toward the other woman Daliah took the mug from her hands and escorted

Mrs. Script to a crate. "You sit there," Daliah said with a smile. "You're boy will be fine as long as you do what I say."

Moving away from Mrs. Script, Daliah sought out the sugar heaping it into the mug and stirring the brew before forcing it back into the other woman's hands. "You drink this while I check the rest of the pot."

"Thank you," Mrs. Script said, tears pouring down her face as the danger of the moment passed and shock set in.

Spencer watched the young woman from his hiding place for a few more moments, thankful that she had joined the wagon train with the Hamptons. She had been a blessing to so many already.

Turning his horse away from the vision of Daliah making Mrs. Script drink her tea and pouring the larger pot of tea into an empty jug to cool, he moved back along the wagons, checking on others.

Daliah looked up from her work catching a glimpse of Mr. Gaines riding on down the line. The wagons would need to roll soon, and she would see to it that the Script family was ready when the call came.

"Trey, you doing all right?" she asked, smiling at the young man who looked like some odd sort of scarecrow with his arms stretched out awkwardly at shoulder height.

"I'll be right back," she added with a smile. "You stay like that until I come back." She smiled, hurrying around the wagon and back to the Hamptons.

A few minutes later, she returned with Orville and together, they quickly hitched the team, prepared the wagon and setting the camp to rights.

"Mrs. Script," she said softly a few minutes later, handing the woman a cookie. "You finish this.

Then I'll show you how to tend to Trey."

"What would we do without you?" Mrs. Script said, draining her cup and taking the cookie. "You've been a godsend."

Daliah blushed slightly. No one had ever been grateful for her before. It was an odd feeling to be needed and wanted. Her whole life had been one change after another, but suddenly she felt like she had a purpose.

"You come with me and we'll dress Trey's injury. You'll need to soak rags in the cold tea three or four times a day and wrap it over the injury. Be careful not to burst the blisters or cause creases with it."

Mrs. Script nodded, listening to every word and nodding her understanding while Daliah demonstrated the skill.

Chapter 11

"Pa, pa," Chad tugged at his father's sleeve, "I'm hungry." the boy groaned.

"What?" Spencer asked as he looked at the slowly sinking sun. He had kept the boy with him all day, keeping him away from old Mr. Franco and trouble. The day had been long and with the weather fine, they had decided to push on to the next good spring and stop for a couple of days.

"We'll stop soon," Spencer said, shaking his head at his own son's appetite. "I swear you eat as much as I do."

"Well, I want to grow up to be big like you," Chad offered sensibly.

Spencer smiled, ruffling the boy's hair. "We'll stop soon," he repeated.

"You could carry me back to old Mrs. Hampton," Chad said hopefully. "She always has something good to eat."

Spencer stiffened in his saddle. He could take the boy back to the last wagon in the line. The

Hamptons had been a blessing with the boy, but he would need to sit with Daliah again if he went there, and he already found the young woman far too interesting.

The more he tried to avoid her, the more he seemed to notice her every move. He noted the glint of sun on her golden locks or the way her hips swung when she walked along beside the wagon.

He even noticed when she seemed pensive or perhaps sad. Although she never hesitated to help others on the drive, she seemed to barely worry about herself.

If Chad was with her, she gave him her full attention, ignoring the dust on her skirt hem or the damp grass soaking her shoes. She had some strange quality about her that drew his eye again and again, and despite himself, Spencer couldn't seem to ignore her.

"Please, Pa, Mrs. Hampton has the best food any-where, and I don't like your cookin' so much no more."

Spencer chuckled, calling himself every kind of a fool as he turned his horse and cantered down the line of wagons toward the end, letting the weary travelers know that they'd be stopping soon.

***

Daliah lifted her eyes from the trail as the sound of a horse traveling at speed caught her ear.

She could see young Chad clinging to the saddle horn, a bright smile on his little face, as his father rode quickly toward the wagon.

"Good evening, Mr. Gaines," she offered politely as he drew up along the wagon. "Are we stopping soon?"

Spencer tipped his hat at the pretty woman who pushed her oversized hat back on her head of golden hair. "Not long now, Miss," he said, meeting her dark gaze.

"Glory be," Mrs. Hampton called from the wagon seat. "I'm about to climb down and lay myself in the cold ground after so long on this seat," the old woman said, making Daliah laugh.

Spencer's lips pulled into a grin and his heart skipped at the lilting sound of Daliah's laugh. She always seemed so serious and self-disciplined the sound surprised him.

"The lead wagons should be reaching the pools about now," Spencer said. "You'll be making camp before long."

"I'm hungry now," Chad grumbled rudely.

"You come on over to the wagon here with Orville and me, Chad," Mrs. Hampton said, reaching for the boy. "I've got a cookie that'll hold you over until we can make some grub."

Chad smiled brightly, knowing that his words had gotten him what he wanted once again even as his father leaned over, letting the boy jump into the wagon box before swinging down from the saddle and drifting back to walk with Miss. Owens.

"I hope today hasn't been too taxing," Spencer said, letting his reins run through his hands.

"No, we aren't moving very fast, so it is easy to keep up."

"I saw you with Mrs. Script's boy earlier. You did real good."

Daliah dropped her eyes back to the ground, the rustling of her skirts and the creak of the wagon wheels the only sound for several seconds.

"My mother taught me about burns," she said simply. "My mother learned from her mother and I learned from both of them at least as long as I had them."

"How long have they been gone?" Spencer asked, the words tumbling from his lips before he realized it.

"Mother has been gone nearly five years, but grandmother passed before we took the trail west."

"I'm sorry," Spencer said, suddenly realizing just how alone this young woman was. She seemed so young to have lost so many loved ones so soon.

"Thank you," Daliah replied softly.

Spencer walked along with Daliah for several more minutes, his mind full of thoughts of his own loss and the shock it had been to him and his son. He'd been lost for months, wandering from place to place doing whatever it took to keep them both fed.

Something flickered in his soul, deep in the depths and barely perceived. Finally, he would have a home in Texas. A new life and a fresh start for both himself and Chad. He only hoped that he could make it stick as he joined his brother. Perhaps being needed by someone else again might hold him in place long enough for his son to grow into a man.

The wagon rolled to a stop without Spencer noticing and he continued forward until a soft hand came to rest on his arm.

"I think we're here, Mr. Gaines," Daliah said quietly, looking up from under the brim of her hat with a smile. "Won't you stay for dinner?"

Chapter 12

Spencer took a seat by the fire next to Mr. Hampton and tried to concentrate on the older man's conversation, but every movement around the fire was a distraction.

Daliah's presence seemed to fill the campfire as she worked to help Mrs. Hampton prepare the evening meal that would be shared with others.

Further, into the small clearing, Mr. Franco was tuning up his fiddle, and a feeling of cheer seemed to permeate the circle of wagons around the glistening spring.

The children's laughter told Spencer that the families were beginning to relax, and he sighed as he mentally counted out the days before they got to Texas.

"Mr. Gaines, Mr. Gaines?" Orville Hampton called. "How long did you say?"

"What?" Spencer pulled his mind back to the conversation with a shake. "I'm sorry, what was that?" he asked sullenly.

"How much longer until we get to this town in Texas?" Orville asked.

"Oh, maybe three weeks if we make good time, four at the outside."

Mr. Hampton smiled. "I'm looking forward to setting up house once we get there. I always enjoyed working with my hands, and I'm not past it yet. I can still wield a hammer as good as anyone. I even brought one of the smaller sawmill blades along under the wagon, so we can set up a mill right quick."

"From what I hear, there's need of men and women who aren't afraid of hard work," Spencer said. "Other than my brother's ranch, there isn't much of a town, and folks are hoping that our wagon train will change the progress and tone of the location."

"Bit rough, huh?" Orville asked, leaning in conspiratorially. "Back when me and Olive started out, things was pretty rough there in Smithfield too, but bit by bit folks made a go of it and look at our former home now."

Spencer smiled, gazing around him at the families getting ready to eat. There were only about ten wagons altogether, very nearly split between single men and families. They had each set out on this journey to find something new, and he hoped it worked out for everyone.

From his brother's latest letter, he knew there was plenty of land to be had in the unnamed town and that skilled labor and trades were lacking from the rolling hills and low fields of the area.

"I think there's plenty of opportunity for anyone willing to put a hand to hard work," Spencer continued. "My brother's ranch is growing. He and his men have been collecting wild cattle from the area and building a herd. They've already put in a cabin and a few huts and a good barn at his place. So I think there's money to be made if folks will try."

Mr. Hampton nodded his head, a bright light in his dark eyes. "It ain't easy starting over, or even starting out," the old man said, "but at least we have a chance, and with a little effort and a load of prayer, we might just turn our new home into something."

Mr. Hampton turned toward the fire and smiled at Daliah as she stirred something in the large dutch oven. "What you makin' tonight?" he asked with a grin.

"Olive is reheating the stew from last night, so I decided we needed something sweet. I'm making brown sugar dumplings just like my mother used to make," she said with a smile.

"That sounds mighty good," Mr. Hampton said, patting his stomach, "this long travel day seems to have left me hollow as an old stump."

Spencer looked up, meeting Daliah's eyes with a grin. The Hampton's had big hearts and their kind and giving nature set everyone at ease. It was no wonder that Daliah fit in so well with them. He wondered if she would stay with them after they arrived in Texas or if one of the single men in the train would get around to courting her.

A flicker of something akin to jealousy raced through his middle like hot lead, and he shoved it away with a growl. He didn't need a woman in his life. He only needed to get Chad settled. Still, something deep inside seemed to wriggle like a butterfly still trapped in its cocoon as he thought of Daliah marrying one of the men they now traveled with.

"What's brown sugar dumplings?" Chad asked, hurrying to the fire as if drawn there by a string. "I want some," he added, reaching toward the heavy pot.

"No," Daliah cried, grabbing the boy's hand before any harm could be done. "It's scorching, Chad," she said softly, pulling the now irritated boy to her. "You could burn yourself and besides, if you open the lid too soon, you'll ruin everyone's dessert."

"Are you sure?" the boy asked. "I'm hungry now."

"You're always hungry," Spencer chided, a mixture of fear, gratitude, and irritation coursing through him. He seldom spoke up to his son, but this time he was sure that only Daliah's quick reflexes had saved him from a terrible scalding.

"He's a growing boy," Daliah said, standing from where she'd bent to talk to Chad. "We'll have supper in a jiffy," she finished placing the boy's hand into his father's larger ones. "Just be patient a little longer."

Spencer looked down into the soft-featured of the young woman as she met his gaze and that little butterfly in his middle seemed to struggle harder to escape its carapace. "Thank you," he said lamely, letting his eyes convey his thoughts.

Daliah looked up into Mr. Gaines's eyes, seeing something there that she didn't recognize. The man had been extra attentive to the Hamptons, and she appreciated the fact. Chad, though often into one scrape or another, made her smile, and she realized that he was missing having a mother to care for him.

Daliah didn't doubt that Mr. Gaines loved his son, but trying to raise the boy on his own had to be complicated.

"Stew's ready," Mrs. Hampton called. "Let's take everything over under the trees and eat."

"Gather round folks, gather round!" Mr. Hampton called. "Bring what you have to share and we'll celebrate this restful place. Olive's brought stew and Daliah has dessert. Tonight we celebrate the blessing of our safety so far," he finished as others came forward, bringing with them what they had to offer. So tonight, no one would go to bed hungry.

Daliah watched as the others filled their plates, chatting and commenting on the bounty that the impromptu dinner had yielded. Then, patiently she dished out spoonfuls of her sticky dessert smiling and nodding at her friends as they found places around a fire to eat.

"I think you've missed someone," Mr. Gaines said, stepping up to her with a plate full of food.

"Oh, I'm sorry, Mr. Gaines, I didn't realize you wanted any," Daliah said, preparing her spoon.

"I was talking about you," he said, handing her the plate. "You need to eat too."

Daliah dropped her eyes, embarrassed at the attention, but Mr. Gaines pressed the plate into her hands. "Thank you."

"Hey, where's my dessert?" Chad called, racing up to his father. "I thought you said I could have some when it was ready?" he continued, glaring at Daliah.

"It's right here," Daliah said, reaching for a tin cup full of fluffy dumplings covered in a smooth brown sugar sauce. "I saved it especially for you."

"You did?" Chad looked up, his bright eyes full of shock. "Why?"

"Because you are my special friend," Daliah said.

Chad dug his fork into his cup of sweets with a shrug. "Okay," he said, shoving a bite of the mixture into his mouth as he walked back toward the other children.

In the background, Mr. Franco began to play a reel, and several couples rose, starting a dance.

Daliah tapped her foot to the music as she ate her meal. More couples stepped out onto the flat grassy plain, moving to the lively tune of the fiddle with delight.

"Why don't you dance, Daliah," Olive said, stepping up to her and Mr. Gaines. "Perhaps Mr. Gaines will be kind enough to take a turn.

Daliah looked up into the handsome face of Spencer Gaines, her heart in her throat as she wondered if he would go along with Olive's request.

As Spencer looked down into the young woman's face seeing a glimmer of hope in her eyes, he couldn't say no.

"I'd be pleased," he said, taking the empty plate from her and handing it to Mrs. Hampton as he led Daliah into the crowd.

***

Daliah placed her hand in Mr. Gaines's rough one as he swung her toward the music, his other hand taking her waist. It had been ages since she'd danced, and her feet felt heavy at first, but the lean man in the dark Stetson moved her smoothly through the step.

"I haven't danced in so long," Daliah said, trying to keep pace with the music. "You must think me useless."

"I think you just need to relax and enjoy the music," Spencer said. Daliah felt so right next to him. He had almost forgotten what it was like to enjoy the company of a woman.

Daliah smiled and the motion flashed into her eyes as she relaxed. Warmth pooled across her back, and the tension that had made her stiff evaporated.

Spencer could see a flicker of joy reach out and touch Daliah, transforming her usually serious face. Had life been so hard that she had forgotten how to smile, how to enjoy the simple things. Instinctively, he pulled her closer, quickening his step as the song whirled toward its end.

Daliah gasped then laughed as Spencer spun her quickly to a standstill, releasing her as everyone clapped for Mr. Franco.

"That seems to have done you some good," Spencer said, not knowing where the words came from. "You should laugh more often."

Daliah ducked her head again as together they walked toward the fire where Mrs. Hampton was handing out cups of coffee.

"I'm afraid I've been a little too busy to dance or laugh," Daliah admitted.

"Life has a way of doing that to us all," Spencer said, thinking of the days that seemed to have passed without his notice.

Chad was growing like a bad weed, and days seemed to come and go with eminent sameness. If he hadn't had his job and his son, he suspected that he would have long ago disappeared into the wilds.

"You look very pensive," Daliah noted, taking a cup from her friend.

"I was just thinking on how life has been very much the same thing day after day, at least until recently."

"Why is that?" Daliah asked, handing him a cup of coffee.

Spencer took the cup, then reached out, taking her elbow and leading her to a stump. "If I didn't know any better, I'd think I had hope."

"What do you hope for?" Daliah asked. This was the first time that she had genuinely carried on a conversation with Mr. Gaines. Before, he had always been polite and grateful for her help with

Chad, but this was different.

"We're getting closer to our goal," Spencer said. "We've had good travel with no more than the usual bad luck, and folks are getting along pretty well."

"You think we'll make it to Texas soon then?"

"Should be a few more weeks," Spencer said.

"What will you do when we get there?" Daliah asked.

Spencer looked up into her pretty face and shrugged. "I'll work on my brother's ranch, I guess."

"Don't you know?"

"Dan said he needed folks to help build the town and work the ranch, so we organized this arrangement to see if we could bring him what he needs," Spencer said, gesturing around him with his mug.

"But what would you like to do?" Daliah asked.

Spencer shrugged again. "I'll just be glad to be settled somewhere. It's time for Chad to have a real home."

"I'm sure he'll like that," Daliah admitted, "and he'll get his pony."

"Yes, he'll get his pony," Spencer agreed with a slight chuckle.

Daliah finished her coffee with a grin then blinked as one of the single men traveling with them stepped up, hat in hand.

"Would you care to dance, Miss Owens?" he asked, the skin around his collar going a delicate pink.

Spencer glared at the younger man, but Daliah rose, taking the outstretched hand as Jim Wallace led her to the dance area.

Something hot rolled over in Spencer's stomach and he growled low in his throat as he pushed the feeling away. It was ridiculous to think of a woman like Daliah as anything but a travel companion, but he seemed to have made some connection with her.

Between her care of others, the help she provided for the Hamptons, and her quiet ways, Daliah had somehow made an impression on him. Still, it was none of his business who she danced with or what she did once they got to the end of the trail. He would work with his brother. No woman would want the rough life offered by a ranch full of wild cowboys and wilder cows.

Daliah tried to carry on a polite conversation with Jim as they made a turn around the dance space but felt stiff and awkward once more. Somehow, Mr. Gaines had been able to put her at ease, but with Mr. Wallace, she felt out of place.

The dance ended, thankfully fast, and Joe wandered away to ask one of the teens in the party for the next round.

"Daliah," Chad tugged at her skirts as she eased back into the shadow of a wagon to catch her breath.

"Yes, Chad?" she said, leaning down to listen to the boy.

"Trey says his arm hurts," the boy said.

"Why don't we go check on him then," Daliah said, taking Chad's hand and heading back the way the boy had come.

Trey Script sat on a barrel, his arm ruched up at an odd angle and a scowl on his face.

"I'm sorry to bother you, Miss Daliah," he said, "but my arm is hurtin' and itchin' something fierce.

"Let me see," Daliah said, concern showing in the wrinkle of her brow as she helped Trey out of his shirt.

"It's a little puckered here," Daliah said, looking at a spot where a blister had collapsed and pressed against the skin. "You'll need to soak it in tea more often," she continued.

"Trey, I've been looking everywhere for you," Mrs. Script called, walking around the wagon. "Oh, Daliah, I'm so glad you're here. I just finished cooling the tea. I got a bit caught up what with all the activity tonight. I think the tea is helping, though."

Daliah smiled at the other woman. "Your timing is perfect," Daliah said softly. "Trey needs to put a compress on this again, so the skin stays soft and smoothes out. Then, wrap it if you need to for the drive tomorrow.

"My mother said it was the tannic acid in the tea that softened the skin and kept it from scaring," she finished.

A few minutes later, Trey was wrapped in tea-soaked rags while his mother fussed over him, and Chad tugged at Daliah's skirt once more.

"You should dance with my pa again," the boy said, turning innocent eyes toward her. "He smiled when you danced before."

Daliah's heart skipped in her breast. Was what the boy said true? Mr. Gaines had been a man of few words and now that she thought of it, he seldom smiled.

Still pondering the statement, Daliah blindly followed Chad across the open space until he stopped in front of his father once more.

"Daliah wants to dance," the boy said, plopping her hand into his father's without warning and making her start.

"Oh dear," Daliah gasped in embarrassment, "I

didn't, I mean Chad, well he said…."

A rough chuckle rumbled from Spencer's chest as he squeezed Daliah's hand. "We might as well humor the boy," he said, rising from his seat and leading her back to the dance area. "It's kind of nice just to enjoy the evening and not think about to-morrow," he added as the music picked up and he whirled his pretty partner around the now dusty circle.

Chapter 13

The dancing lasted into the night as people unwound, releasing the cares of their road-weary days, and laughter was common on the night air.

Freshwater, good grazing for stock, and the pulling together of a community lifted spirits as much as knowing they would have a full day of rest on the morrow.

As campfires burned down and children were tucked in for the night, Spencer walked the camp checking for trouble as he tried to settle his busy mind.

Spencer had enjoyed his dances with Miss Owens far more than he would like to admit and couldn't help but smile at how his son had wrangled her into another dance with him. As one of the leaders of the train, Spencer tried to keep himself distant from people in case some conflict arose, but he had to admit that he gravitated toward the Hamptons and the young lady traveling with him.

Was he starting to like Daliah? He pondered the

question as he gazed up into a star-lit sky. He could admit he admired her. She had been a constant help to anyone who had suffered even a minor injury as the wagon train had steadily wound southwest toward their goal. Her quiet nature and soft voice put people at ease, somehow filling them with confidence as she worked toward easing their pain.

The young woman with the dark eyes and golden locks was hard-working, and he had never heard her complain even after the longest day of travel. Spencer wasn't sure if the Hamptons would have fared nearly as well if the young woman hadn't accompanied them on this journey. True, they were still strong and healthy for their age, but they were no longer young.

Settling on a stump near the glistening spring,

Spencer removed his hat, running his fingers through his dark locks, then looked back toward the heavens as if seeking some answer he couldn't find on his own.

Daliah Owens was a mystery to him. Was she a young woman following the Hamptons because she had nowhere else to go, or was there some credence to the rumors he had heard about her and her dismissal from her job at the bank a few short months ago?

No matter how Spencer worried about the problem, he couldn't match the young woman he had come to know with any shred of those rumors. She seemed to be precisely what you saw. A lone young woman, doing her best to survive in a world that could be sometimes as cruel as it was beautiful. Even if she had made mistakes along the way, didn't everyone? The west was a place for hope and new beginnings. What was past should stay in the past.

Spencer dropped his head as his thoughts pricked his heart. Hadn't he been holding on to the anger and bitterness of his loss? Instead, he'd allowed the pain of losing his wife to cloud his heart and mind, making life the simple drudgery of survival, work, and care.

The wall around the lean man's heart seemed to crack and shatter as he realized he had been going through the motions of life without actually living.

Rising, he gazed at the stars one more time, twirling his hat in his hand as a heavyweight eased from his heart. Then, with a smile, he turned back to his fire to check on Chad. Tomorrow was a new start for both of them.

***

Daliah wrapped herself in her bedroll under the wagon and peered out at the bright stars above. The smell of wood smoke and prairie grass filled her nostrils as the cold air of evening began to descend upon the quiet camp.

Her mind drifted back to Mr. Gaines and the dances they had shared that night. She had danced with a few of the other men in the train that evening but had ended up in Mr. Gaines's arms at the end of the night.

She smiled, remembering the feeling of his strong hands on her waist and the smile that played across his face as they had glided over the ground. For the first time in many months, even years, Daliah felt safe when Mr. Gaines took her into his arms.

Daliah had been devastated after the loss of her parents, but having her older brother, her security, her safety had gotten her through that. Together they had clung to God and His promises as they had moved on mourning yet trying to live the life they were meant to have.

When her brother had died, Daliah's world had shattered into a million pieces, and if not for the kindness of the Hamptons and the desperate realization that she must work or starve, Daliah feared she might have given up completely. It was as if she had been hanging on a high wire looking down at a crowd far below, and someone had ripped her safety net away.

Now, even after years of living without him, Daliah still missed the energetic, self-confident and dedicated assurance of her brother's presence.

Gazing at the stars above, a soft smile flickered across Daliah's full lips as she thought of her family, her heart filled with a gentle love that seemed to drown out the bitter pain of loss. As her eyes picked out the brightest stars in the heavens, she thought of each tiny flickering light as a remembrance even while her mind turned back to Mr. Gaines and young Chad.

"God, I know I'm not much account on this earth. I haven't lived as well as others and I'm only a simple girl, but I pray for Mr. Gaines and young Chad. I pray that you will watch over them and keep them safe and bring them to this new home where they might find love and peace." She paused, gazing more closely at the stars and picking out the constellations her brother had taught her so long ago. "Amen," she whispered as she closed her eyes and drifted into a peaceful sleep.

Chapter 14

The extra day of rest near fresh water and good feed was exactly what the party needed as they rolled out onto the prairie at the crack of dawn a day later with bright smiles and rested bodies.

A golden sun was peaking over the eastern horizon as the wagons trundled across the dusty prairie toward the promise of hope, home, and happiness.

Daliah lifted her face to the warmth of a new day like a daisy turning its yellow head toward God. She was clean, warm, and well-fed, and her heart was filled with the hope of a brighter future.

The sound of a galloping horse made her smile as she caught a glimpse of Mr. Gaines riding toward her.

"Chad asked if he could walk along with you a bit," the man said, meeting her gaze. "Would you mind?"

"I'd count it a privilege," Daliah said with a grin as Spencer swung his son into the dew-drenched grass. "I'll see you at lunch," he said. "You mind Miss Owens," he finished touching his hat politely then wheeling and galloping toward the front of the line.

"Aren't you tired of walkin' all the time?" Chad said, trudging along beside her. "Maybe you could ride along with my pa sometime if your feet get tired."

Daliah suppressed a giggle at the boy's words. "I think I'd take up more room on your pa's horse than would be good," she said instead. "Besides, I like walking."

"You do?"

"Yes, it gives me time to think."

"About what?"

"Everything," Daliah answered, stretching her arm to encompass the prairie. "I think about where we're going and what it will be like there. I think about my family and friends, and sometimes I talk to God."

The boy shot her an odd look making her grin again. "Does God answer?" he asked.

"In His way, yes."

"How?"

Daliah lifted her head, looking at the wagon on her right. "One example is when I had nowhere to go and no one to look after me. I asked God to show me which way to go and then the Hamptons invited me to join them. That was one answer."

"I don't think Pa talks to God," Chad admitted. "He's quite like, most days."

"I'm sure he's busy keeping us all safe as we travel," Daliah said.

"He had fun last night, though," Chad said. "I think he enjoyed dancing. I liked your dumplings best, is what I liked."

Daliah laughed, looking down at the boy with affection. The scamp was as likely to be found dozing in someone's wagon as throwing stones at a jackrabbit on any given day. He could find trouble in a heartbeat, but she felt a kinship to him just the same.

"Maybe I'll make some more dumplings when we get closer to our new home," Daliah offered. "We'll celebrate."

"Can I go play with Trey?" Chad asked, suddenly looking along the line of wagons toward the boy he admired so.

"Why don't I take you up there myself," Daliah said. "I'll see if Trey is feeling better today."

"Okay," Chad replied, skipping on ahead as Daliah lifted her skirts, hurrying to keep up.

They found Trey driving his mother's team of

oxen with a short prod and an easy way. The young man had taken on a great deal of responsibility as the man of the family as they traveled toward where his father was getting ready to set up a store.

"Hi Trey," Chad called, stepping up to the older boy. "What ya doing?"

Trey smiled. "The same thing I've been doing for nearly two months," the young man said. "Driving the team, 'course I'm also trying not to itch under my arm at the same time," he added, grinning at Daliah.

"Sounds like that burn is healing then," the young woman said. "I'm glad. Is there any trouble moving it?"

"Nah," Trey replied, shifting his prod and rotating his arm in every direction he could think of.

"Oh Daliah," Mrs. Script hurried around the back of the wagon. "Trey's doing just fine," she said, relief evident in her eyes. "Mr. Gaines said we might make it to our stopping point in three weeks if the weather holds, and we don't have any more troubles," she continued, a cheery tone in her voice.

"You're meeting your husband in the no-name town we're headed to, aren't you?" Daliah asked.

"I am," Mrs. Script said, a bright smile covering

her face. "William took a job on a steamboat delivering supplies to folks along the river, and when he saw the place, he decided to stop and find us a new start."

"I'm looking for the same thing," Daliah said, falling into step with Mrs. Script as they followed the wagon smiling as Trey helped Chad into the wagon to rest his legs.

"Do you know what to expect in our new home?" Daliah asked. She couldn't help but worry about how she and the Hamptons would be making a living. Perhaps she could cook in the camp for single men or take a job washing on a ranch.

"Do you smell smoke?" Trey asked as the heavy oxen lumbered along the trail.

The sound of horses thundering along the trail startled all of them as Mr. Gaines and Ben raced toward them shouting.

"Fire! Fire!" Spencer called, his heart pounding in his chest. He had spotted the prairie fire racing their way as he'd been out scouting the trail. It was still a few miles away, but with the wind sweeping this way, it would be here soon.

Daliah looked up, fear closing her throat as she reached for Chad, pulling him roughly from the wagon seat.

"We have to get to the Hamptons," she shouted

as Trey blinked. "You too," she added, grabbing Mrs. Script. "Trey, turn the oxen loose and run for the Hamptons wagon!"

"Give me, Chad," Spencer yelled, sliding to a stop in a shower of twigs and dust.

"Turn the Oxen loose!" his voice raised to be heard along the line. They'll have to run. Get into the horse-drawn wagons!" his voice cracked.

People scrabbled, fear making their motions jolting as panicked tears began to fall.

Daliah raced to the Hamptons pushing Mrs. Script into the wagon as Trey climbed into the seat next to Olive.

"Wildfire!" she yelled, pointing toward Mr. Gaines' lathered horse. "Follow him and grab anyone you can along the way!"

Mr. Hampton clutched the lines in his hands, turning the horses toward Mr. Gaines, who was directing the over full wagons pulled by four hitch horse teams as smoke reached the edge of the prairie within view.

"Hold on," the old man shouted, lashing the reins across the horses' rumps and heading away from the blaze.

Daliah wrapped her arms around Mrs. Script as the wagon lurched into a jostling run, bouncing and jumping over uneven ground as it raced to safety.

Behind her, through the canvas cover of the wagon, she could see other teams charging behind, the lesser horses racing at top speed as their drivers and fear drove them forward. Around them, heavy oxen free from their cumbersome burdens bawled, wild-eyed as they charged away from danger in the wake of the wagons.

"My wagon," Mrs. Script sobbed as behind them, an angry glow engulfed all that had been left behind.

Ahead of them, Daliah could hear Mr. Gaines shouting, encouraging the wagons to greater speed. He'd spotted a trickle of a stream a mile in the distance, and their only hope was to cross the creek before the leaping tongues of flame reached them.

Mr. Hampton lashed at his team, his voice a ragged prayer as the horses plunged down the steep slope toward the water, splashing across the stream then dragging on the reins to pull the horses into a long arch as others followed.

As the wagon slowed, Daliah leapt from the back, racing to the stream where the last wagon rocked, nearly tipping as it struggled across, the tail of the wagon sparking into flame as the wind shifted cinders onto the canvas.

Stumbling as the wagon continued, Daliah

grabbed a bucket and plunged back into the stream filling the bucket and throwing it onto the smoldering cover where children stared out in tear-washed fear. Another bucket splashed from the other side as friends and neighbors hurried to drown flames on the still moving wagon.

Struggling up the now muddy bank, the last wagon staggered to a stop. The weary travelers watched as the dry grass of the prairie on the other side of the stream was consumed by lashing tongues of flame.

Daliah brushed her hand across her face smearing the dark smudge of soot on her forehead then hurried to the wagon to check on the children.

Several of the smaller ones were clinging to their mothers, while men did their best to tend to over-stressed stock and take inventory of their rigs.

Shock, fear, and adrenaline permeated the small gathering as Mr. Gaines, and Mr. Ben rode around the camp trying to calm jangled nerves.

"Where's my stock?" Trey called, his eyes red from the smoke that drifted across the shallow stream as the fire crept further down the path they had just covered. "Has anyone seen my stock?" he asked again, wiping moisture from reddened eyes.

"Most of them seem to be here on our side," Mr. Gaines called, gazing around them from his vantage point on horseback, his voice steady as he approached the boy. "They followed the wagons. We'll round them up again, son."

Trey nodded, wiping his eyes on a sleeve as he turned to help his shivering mother from the Hampton wagon.

"Daliah, take Chad," Spencer said, not realizing he had used the young woman's Christian name. "I'll see what I can do to round up the stock and check on everyone."

He was gone before Daliah could reply as she lowered his son to the ground.

"Did everything burn up?" Chad asked, still holding to her hand. "Will we have to walk from now on?"

"No, Chad, everything didn't burn up," Daliah replied, praying that it was true, "and even if it did, there are enough of us left to see us into Texas."

"You think so?" Mrs. Script asked. "You think anything could have survived that?"

Daliah wrapped her arm around the other woman moving the little troop toward the front of the wagon where Mr. Hampton and Trey were unhitching the heaving, sweat lathered team.

"I'm starting some tea and biscuits," Mrs. Hampton said, straightening her bonnet that had hung crookedly down her back. "We can all use a good strong cup of tea to settle our nerves," she added, her hands shaking as she tied the bonnet in place.

"Will you help Olive?" Daliah asked, walking Mrs. Script to the stove that Mrs. Hampton had unloaded from the wagon. "I'm going to check in on everyone."

Turning, Daliah walked among her shaken friends calling the younger single men to tend the horses as she moved women and children toward Mrs. Hampton's heavy kettle that was starting to steam.

There had been several bruises and abrasions during the rough and terrifying drive to cross the stream, but thankfully, no one had been seriously injured, and at least half of the wagons that had made it to safety were undamaged.

"Miss Owens?" Spencer called to the young woman as she finished bandaging a scraped elbow. "Would you mind coming with me?" the trail boss asked, his eyes serious.

"Of course," Daliah said, worry coursing through her like a shock of lightning. "Is anything wrong?"

"It's my partner Ben. He's not feeling well after that ride, says his arm hurts something fierce."

Daliah stopped in her tracks, looking up to meet Spencer's eyes. "I need something from the wagon," she said, not waiting on his reply as she lifted her skirts and ran.

Spencer waited impatiently for Daliah to catch up again. She was out of breath, but she didn't slow down until they reached Ben at the lead wagon, where the older man sat propped against a wheel.

"He doesn't look so good," Daliah said, opening a small carpetbag she had brought with her and examining the older trail boss. His pale, waxy skin made her fear that they were too late. "I'm not trained for this sort of thing, but my mother said that these are signs that the heart isn't working properly. I could help him or hurt him," she finished pleading with Spencer with her eyes.

"Do whatever you can," Spencer said. "Ben is a good man. He deserves to see his new home."

Daliah nodded, reaching into the bag, pulling out a tiny bottle, and dropping the smallest bit of liquid onto Ben's tongue. The man's eyes fluttered open as she eased him to the ground and undid the top buttons of his shirt.

"If it is going to work, we'll know soon," Daliah said, lifting a silent prayer to heaven that she had done the right thing.

"I'm going after the rest of the stock," Spencer said, handing a blanket down to Daliah. "We can't do anything without those oxen. Will you be all right?"

"I'll be fine," Daliah said. "Go with God."

Spencer threw himself into the saddle then trotted toward Ben's horse that was nibbling grass near the wagon. Then, grabbing the other mounts reins, he headed for the wagons calling for young Trey.

"How is he, dear?" Mrs. Hampton startled Daliah as she walked up to her a few minutes later. "Mr. Gaines mentioned what happened and asked if I'd check in on you. So I brought you a cup of tea," the old woman finished handing the steaming mug to Daliah.

"He seems to be breathing easier," Daliah said. "Isn't it strange that we've been on the trail for nearly two months, and I barely know this man?" she asked.

"I believe Mr. Ben usually does the scouting and hunting," Olive said. "He keeps himself to himself."

Daliah nodded, looking off toward the blackened plain on the other side of the stream. The fire had raced on, hopefully dying when it hit the spring they had camped at the night before but leaving behind a charred desolate landscape in its wake.

"Do you think anything is left?" she asked, looking up at Mrs. Hampton.

"I don't know, dear," the older woman replied.

"The fire was moving fast, and if the wind shifted, perhaps the wagons won't be gone. All we can do now is pray and plan for what comes next."

***

An hour's rest for the stock and everyone loaded back into the wagons turning back to see what could be salvaged from the wagon's that had been left behind. Placing old Ben into the Hampton's wagon, Spencer looked at Daliah, nodding as he met her dark gaze.

"Thank you for looking after him," he said simply before swinging up onto his horse and turning back across the stream.

They were heading back to where the other wagons had been abandoned with hopes and prayers in their hearts that something would be left of the life so many were trying to build.

Chapter 15

Daliah lifted her head, her mouth and nose covered with a damp bandana, and gazed out across the blackened prairie. In the distance, the canvas covers of the abandoned wagons rippled in the wind giving her heart hope.

The closer they came, the more they could see of the damage the wildfire had caused. Charred wheels and fire black wagon tongues blended with the stark bareness of the earth, filling them all with a mixture of hope and trepidation.

"It don't look too bad," Trey said as he drove his nervous team of oxen back toward the wagons. "We might not have no real trouble," the young man's optimism was contagious and others quickened their steps.

"Don't look like any of the rigs is burned up," Mr. Jostens said. "The wood's a mite blackened but not burnt. The wind must have took the fire across too fast to get a bite," he added with a grin, squeezing his wife's hand.

"I hear some folks blacken wood on their

wagons and homes to make 'em more waterproof anyhow," another of the single drivers called, taking a turn around his own rig.

"Check your trees and collars carefully," Spencer called, handing Chad down to Daliah without even asking. "If it's in good knick, get hitched up and we'll head out to a good spot to let the stock graze."

Men, women, and boys all scrabbled to get the nervy stock hooked up and test the soundness of their wagons. It was a miracle in itself that none of the precious animals had been lost. If the wagons were sound, this would be a day to thank the good Lord for His mercies.

"Ma, you go check the canvas and our supplies," Trey called as he led the four oxen to the wagon and set them into the long tree with their yokes. The boy had somehow had the presence of mind to raise his wagon tongue, saving it from the worst of the flame.

"I think everything is all right," Mrs. Script called. "I'll be glad to be away from this blasted earth, though," she added. "It gives me the shakes, even if it is a miracle that all of our earthly possessions were spared."

"Can I ride in the wagon with you?" Chad asked Daliah as he walked along with her once the wagons were moving again.

"You can ride with the Hamptons," Daliah replied. "I'll walk and look after Mr. Ben."

"You're gonna walk through this?" the boy asked, his bright eyes wide.

"I am," Daliah replied. "The wagon is already heavy enough and the horses are tired."

Chad scratched at his ear for a moment, thinking. "Maybe I'll walk a bit too," he finally said, making Daliah smile. Perhaps the boy was learning something in all of this.

Everyone was nervous as the snorting and stomping oxen leaned into their yokes and started the damaged wagons along the trail. Each creak of wood, each roll of an iron ringed wheel, was watched with bated breath as the travelers set out on the trail. With minutes rolling into an hour, the troupe began to breathe more easily, especially as they finally made their way out of the charred ground and onto the green prairie once more.

"We'll stop here for the night," Spencer called, waving his hand in a circle to indicate they were stopping for the night.

Wearily, the wagons were turned in on themselves and the stock let loose into the makeshift corral made by linked wagons.

"That was the longest day of my life," Olive Hampton said. "I hope we don't have any more drama before we get to our new home."

Daliah wrapped the older woman in her arms, "I couldn't agree more," she said, hugging her tight. "I'm just going to check on Mr. Ben. Then I'll help with supper."

"Oh, I didn't see you ride up," Daliah said, stepping around to the back of the wagon to find Mr. Gaines already there.

"I thought I'd stop and look in on Ben before I checked the camp," Spencer said, twirling the tip of his reins as his horse stood cow-hipped behind him.

"Spence, that you?" Ben called his voice craggy.

"I'm here, Ben," Spencer called. "How you feelin' old man?"

"Like I have one of those fine horses of Mr. Hampton's sitting on my chest," the man replied with a ragged chuckle.

"I'll fetch you some water," Daliah said, hurrying to get a mug.

"What happened Spence," Ben asked.

"Miss Owens thinks your heart gave out on ya," Spencer replied, not holding anything back.

"Can't say I'm surprised," the other man said. "Doctor a few towns back told me about the same. Said I needed to settle down and take it easy if I expected to see another winter."

"Why didn't you tell me?" Spencer said.

"What for," Ben said, his dark eyes boring into his partner. "You got enough to worry about with that boy of yours, and I've been pullin' my own weight, haven't I?"

"I'm just glad you ain't dead," Spencer said. With Ben's help, he had moved three wagon trains to various states across the United States over the years and counted the quiet man a friend.

"Everyone make it?" Ben asked.

"Yes, and not much damage to the wagons we had to leave behind."

Ben smiled, coughing slightly. "I'm glad this is our last trail together," he said. "I'm looking forward to a quiet town and a comfortable rocking chair. As for you, you should get at and marry that girl that's been helping you with Chad. I see the way you look at her, so don't sass," he finished just as Daliah returned with a cool cup of water.

Climbing into the wagon and propping the older man upon a flour sack, Daliah helped him drink, then rummaged for the medicine with one hand as she took his wrist between her fingers. It was apparent that something had passed between the two men by the way that Mr. Gaines was looking at her, but she didn't speak.

"I'll get my horse put up and take a turn around

the camp," Spencer said, his eyes lingering on Daliah a moment longer before he turned, disappearing into the circle of wagons.

"That's a good man there," Ben said.

"Yes, sir," Daliah agreed, giving him the medicine she had.

"I got pills," he said after taking what she offered. "Doc, a few towns back gave 'em to me."

"You still need to rest," Daliah chided.

"I'll slow down, I reckon. Maybe take over driving me and Spence's wagon and let that boy ride ahead a bit."

Daliah smiled. "That sounds like a good plan."

"Does, doesn't it?" Ben said. "I hope you have plans too," he continued. "Like settling down and maybe helping Spence figure out how he belongs in this new place."

"Mr. Gaines?" Daliah said. "What do I have to do with him?"

"He needs help with that boy of his and you got no one but the Hampton's to see to you," Ben said. "You two would do all right together."

"I don't think Mr. Gaines is interested in anything like that," Daliah tried, dropping her eyes and hoping he didn't see the spark of hope in them.

"Spencer has some silly notions in his head yet.

That don't mean any of them amount to a hill of beans," Ben continued, with a slight cough.

Daliah smiled. "You should rest before supper," she said, changing the subject. "I'll come back and fetch you if you're up to it then."

Ben chuckled as the young woman climbed back out of the wagon. He'd given both parties something to think about and that was good enough for now.

***

"Pa, is Ben gonna be all right?" Chad asked as they sat down to dinner around a small campfire, closely watched by all.

"Miss Owens thinks he has a good chance," Spencer replied. "He needs to rest a bit, so don't you go bothering him."

"I thought she was kinda mean when I first met her," Chad said. "She didn't give me that hat, ya know."

"And now?" Spencer asked.

"I like her, and I really like her brown sugar dumplings."

Spencer's bark of laughter made several of the people around the fire look at him oddly, but for once, he didn't care. His son's words had broken the tension that had wound around his middle like steel bands since the fire had caught them, and for the first time that day, he felt like he could breathe again.

Tonight Spencer Gaines was grateful that everyone had survived one of the terrors of the wide-open prairie, and when he made it to Texas, he was determined to settle somewhere that had good water.

Daliah looked across the fire at Mr. Gaines, Ben's words still echoing in her brain as she fixed the older man a plate. She hadn't even thought of the possibility of marriage and family. For far too long, life had been nothing more than going to work and getting through each day on her own.

The Hamptons had been the biggest blessing in her life, and she would always be grateful for their kindness, but she couldn't count on them forever.

Over the past few weeks, she could see changes in Mr. Gaines' attitude toward her. He was less sharp, more willing to talk, and slower to hurry off with a harsh word. Still, she couldn't see the man being interested in a wife or family. Most days, he was still terse and distant. Of course, dancing with him, everything had been so different.

"What's worryin' you?" Ben asked as she carried him a plate. Mr. Hampton had helped the man out of the wagon earlier, letting him sit on a crate against the tailgate, but neither of them thought he should walk more than he had to.

DALIAH

"Excuse me?" Daliah asked, handing him the plate where he sat on the lid of a barrel.

"You look like you got something worryin' you."

"No, I think everyone is just a little overtired and still frightened," Daliah hedged.

"If you say so," Ben smiled, taking a bite of his dinner. "What do you plan on doing once we get to where we're going?" he asked after finishing his first bite.

"I don't know," Daliah admitted.

"You can cook. Might be a need for that some-where, or maybe one of them cowboys will take a fancy to you and marry ya."

"Have you ever been married, Mr. Ben?" Daliah asked, turning the tables on the man.

"Me? No, no. I've got too much of the gypsy in my soul. No woman would want to have lived their life on the trail with me."

Daliah smiled, thinking she'd turned the man away from the track his conversation had been heading. "You never know there might be a woman with an adventuresome soul."

Ben chuckled. "I'm an old man now and looking forward to sitting on the front porch and watch-ing others do for a bit. Them folks you're with," Ben continued waving his fork in the direction of the Hamptons, "they could start up another boarding house or such if you want to live as a spinster lookin' after others."

Daliah bristled at the words. Even if marriage had not been on her mind, no woman liked to be considered a spinster. She was only twenty now as it was. Not quite on the shelf yet.

"I think it's a good thing women like you and some of these families are making this trip," Ben continued as if he hadn't said anything offensive. "Young towns are wild, sometimes dangerous. When folks start making something of it, that's when it will grow up."

"You think where we're going will be dangerous?"

Daliah asked, suddenly worried.

"Not if good folks are determined to make something of it," Ben said, tucking into his dinner with some energy.

Daliah walked back to the fire, thoughts racing through her mind. What would her future hold when she arrived in the no-name town of Texas?

Chapter 16

The next two weeks of travel brought the wagon train closer to its goal, but with changes along the way.

Trey Script took over the work that Ben had been doing while Ben's hired driver took his team of oxen, and Ben took up the traces to the wagon he and Spencer had brought along that had been driven by their hired help.

The days grew warmer the further south they moved, and each stop at a spring was even more appreciated than before.

Spencer dropped Chad off with Daliah each day and ate at the Hampton's each night. But, no matter how hard he tried, he couldn't get the idea of what Ben had said out of his thoughts.

If he were honest, he rather liked the young woman. She didn't seem to think about herself as much as others, a rare quality, and the quiet peacefulness that seemed to emanate around her was refreshing.

Perhaps once he got to town, he might consider calling on Daliah Owens. He did need someone to look after Chad while he was on the range with his brother, after all.

"You're very quiet tonight," Daliah commented as she helped serve dinner one night along the trail. "Are you worried about the trail ahead?"

"Not so much," Spencer admitted. "We've got one more river crossing, but the weather has been good, so I don't see any trouble with it. I imagine you'll be glad to stop traveling soon."

Daliah smiled, appreciating his kind words. "I will," she said. "It has been a long journey." Her mind flashed back to everything that had happened over the past few years, and she prayed this would be the last time she would have to move.

Spencer looked up at the young woman and suddenly realized what he recognized in her. Loss had left her lonely, even among friends. She was a help and a blessing to the Hamptons as much as they were to her, but she had no real anchor on this earth, and something inside him turned, recognizing his own lonely heart.

"It's hard being on your own, isn't it?" he asked quietly, leading her away from the fire to a seat.

Daliah looked up into the man's blue eyes and simply nodded. "I'm afraid I don't know where my place is," she admitted something compelling her

DALIAH

to speak honestly.

Spencer looked at Daliah, fully for the first time since they had danced weeks ago. She was an attractive woman, kind, and hard-working, but there was more to her than that. She had somehow found an inner strength drawn from heaven that kept her moving forward day by day.

For several minutes Daliah sat with Mr. Gaines. They were both silent, but neither seemed to need to speak. Something had changed between them. Something that had been growing as they had connected on the drive. It wasn't something she could put into words, but it was a quiet, solid bond that had sprung from mutual respect and need.

Daliah looked over at Spencer as he finished his meal and smiled. Could she venture to give her heart to Mr. Spencer Gaines? Could she risk loving someone who could be gone in an instant? Perhaps she had been moving toward this all along?

"Daliah, I have a great deal of respect for you, and I can't thank you enough for all of your help, both with Chad and with the troubles we've seen on this trip. I just wanted you to know that," Spencer finished.

"That's very kind of you, Mr. Gaines," Daliah said. "I only do what I can."

"No, you do more than that," Spencer said. "You care about people. We need more of that in this

123

world."

"You and Chad are easy to care about," Daliah whispered, realizing that it was true.

Spencer chuckled, taking her hand and placing it on his arm. "Would you mind going for a walk?" he asked.

Daliah nodded, rising and following him out and around the wagons. Inside the circle of the wagons, the stock grazed quietly or rested, and Daliah realized that soon this journey would end and a new one would start. A journey of finding her place in this world.

"I'm afraid I wasn't very fair to you when we started this journey," Spencer said. "You were trying to be kind and help me with Chad, and I was short and surly with you. I didn't want to be around any woman that reminded me of my wife."

"I remind you of your wife?" Daliah said, looking up in shock, her heart going out to the man.

"Not in appearance, only in determination. My wife was a good woman, and she understood my weaknesses far more than I did. I'm quick to anger and slow to forgive," he continued. "I've been mighty angry with God for a long time, but I'm starting to see that I'm not the only one who has lost and been left adrift on this earth. I kept running when Chad was little, leaving him for months on end with family or friends. Everything has changed on this trip. I'm starting over in a new home with a new life. I'd like to see if perhaps our starting overs could go hand in hand if you're willing." He finished stopping to look down into her face and waiting for some reply.

Daliah was quiet for several heartbeats as she explored her heart. She knew she liked Mr. Gaines now that they had gotten better acquainted. At first, he had put her off, but now she understood how his broken heart had needed time to heal, something she could identify with.

"I think I'd like that," she finally replied, delighted when he smiled.

Spencer felt as if some heavyweight had been lifted from his shoulders as he faced a new future head-on for the first time. For too long, he had been letting the hurt of the past cloud his future. No one was promised tomorrow, something he and the young woman standing next to him knew better than many. Today he would step out in faith and hope that a brighter future waited on the other side.

***

"Daliah, are you gonna marry my pa?" Chad asked a week later as the wagons trundled over the northern border of Texas. They were several days from Dallas but thankfully would reach their new home before that city.

Daliah chuckled, a pink tinge gracing her cheeks. "Your pa and I are just getting to know each other," Daliah said. The past week had been full of more light and laughter than she could remember in many years.

It was as if once Spencer had decided that he could take the risk, he left the shackles of his past behind and was a different person.

Each evening he took Daliah for a turn around the camp while the Hamptons chatted with Ben and their neighbors about where they were going, while Chad played with other children or followed Trey around like a puppy.

"Well, if you decide you like him good enough, I'd be all right with you marryin' him." The boy finished making Daliah laugh.

"Thank you for your permission," Daliah said, ruffling the boy's hair.

"If you do marry my pa, will you make brown sugar dumplings every night and let me eat all of them?"

Daliah's laughter echoed out over the wagon train as it approached the river Spencer had mentioned earlier. "I don't think I can make them every night, and if you eat all of them, you'll get sick, but I could make them sometimes as a treat."

"If you say so," Chad replied, kicking the dust

of the trail with his feet. "I'm gonna go look at the river," he added, trotting off toward the lead wagons that were splashing across the blue trickle.

"Be careful," Daliah called after him, hefting her skirts and hurrying to catch up. She'd already had to fish him out of a stream once before and didn't want to have to do it again.

As she approached the bubbling stream, she smiled at Trey, who sat on Ben's horse in the middle of the knee-deep stream, watching the wagons trundle across the wide bed and up the other side.

"Hey Daliah," Trey called with a wave.

"Hi Trey," Chad called, walking to the stream and sticking his bare feet into the shallows.

"Be careful, Chad," Trey called back. "It gets deeper in the middle.

Daliah smiled across the gap between the wagons at Spencer, who sat on his horse on the other side of the stream. The once stern-looking man waved back with a grin just as a loud splash met her ears.

Turning, Daliah saw Chad topple into the stream, rolling into the current with the downward motion of the stream.

"Chad!" she yelled, rushing into the stream and grabbing the boy, pushing him to shore as her skirt snagged on a hidden log, and she went under the swift-moving waters of the stream.

Trying to un-snag her skirt, Daliah felt herself lose her footing and splash into the faster-moving water. Taking a deep breath, she yanked her hemline free, only to be swept downstream, her head striking a rock as she moved toward the churning feet of the next team.

Spencer choked as he saw Daliah go under, then tumble across the gravelly streambed toward the wagon, then disappear into a deep basin on the edge of the ford before popping up almost under the horse's feet.

A loud whinny made the driver look up, pulling his team to a stop in the middle of the stream as something tumbled under their prancing feet and out the other side.

Spencer was in the water, his hands grasping the sodden dress and pulling Daliah up from the water. Her dress was soaked, her hair hanging over her bloodied face like the long grasses at the edge of the stream.

"Daliah, Daliah," he croaked. "Help," he called as someone reached for him, pulling him and his burden toward the far shore.

"Put her down, son," Mr. Hampton said soothingly, coaxing him to lower Daliah to the earth as Olive stroked the hair from their young boarder's face.

"Daliah," Mrs. Hampton called, checking the bump on the young woman's head then leaning in to see if she was breathing.

"Please God, please no," Spencer groaned as he looked down at the limp form of the woman he was losing his heart to.

"Pa, is Daliah dead?" Chad asked as Trey dropped him from his saddle. "Please don't let Daliah be dead," the boy said, his eyes filling with tears. "I promise I'll be good."

Spencer pulled his boy into his arms, clutching him tight. He could have lost them both.

"She's breathing," Mrs. Hampton said, and Spencer filled his own lungs with air once more.

"Bring her to the wagon," the older woman said. "Trey, you get the rest of them wagons across and we'll stop for the night." She finished as Spencer followed her to the wagon, Daliah resting limp in his arms.

"Don't worry, son," Mr. Hampton said, laying his hand on the man's shoulders. "God didn't bring her this far to end it here. She has work to do yet."

Spencer paced the small patch of dirt next to the wagon for the next fifteen minutes until Olive Hampton climbed from the wagon.

"She wants to see you and the boy," Olive said

with a relieved smile.

Spencer grabbed Chad, pulling him into his arms and climbing into the back of the wagon.

"Let me see Chad," Daliah said, her voice raw and scratchy.

"I'm here, Daliah," Chad said, placing a kiss on her forehead. "I'm sorry I almost got you killed," the boy added with a sniff.

Daliah struggled to reach for the scamp and Spencer slipped his arms behind her helping her sit up as she pulled Chad in for a hug.

"You scared us pretty bad," Spencer said, stroking a stray bit of straw-colored hair from her eyes. "I'd rather you didn't do that anymore," he continued. "I was kinda thinking we might get married when we get to town, ya see."

Daliah smiled, but the action made her head hurt. "So soon?" she asked, lying back against the sacks and pillows.

"After what just happened, I don't want to wait," Spencer admitted. "I didn't see it coming, Daliah Owens, but I've fallen in love with you and I'd like to marry you if you'll have me."

Daliah looked up into Spencer's eyes, setting her heart free to fly to the man who had become so important to her. She could love him if God allowed, and deep down, she knew she already did.

Life was too uncertain to wait when she knew her heart. Closing her eyes, she lifted a prayer of thanks to God, only to pop them open a moment later as Spencer brushed his lips across her lips.

"Yuk!" Chad said. "I don't want to see that," the boy chided, scooting out of the wagon. "I'm getting changed."

Daliah and Spencer chuckled as he squeezed her hand. "I'll let you rest," he said, kissing her one more time as his heart soared.

"All settled," Mrs. Hampton asked Spencer as he climbed out of the wagon, her dark eyes full of a knowing light.

"I guess so," Spencer said, still smiling.

"Good, then I'll help Daliah get into some dry things, and we'll find a preacher as soon as we get settled," she finished with a smile.

Chapter 17

The following day Daliah was still a little light-headed as she rose, dressed, and headed out to help get breakfast started. She still couldn't believe that Spencer had come to love her. How it had happened seemed a mystery to her, but she knew that her heart was drawn to him, and for the first time, her life seemed to have the hope of a future of more than working to keep body and soul together.

"How are you this morning?" Olive asked as she motioned Daliah to a seat where she could stir the oatmeal.

"I'm hopeful," Daliah admitted. "I can't believe that Mr. Gaines cares for me, but he does."

"It was only a matter of time, dear," Mrs. Hampton said, stopping and placing a hand on Daliah's face. "You're a lovely young woman with a big heart, and you deserve some happiness in this world."

A tear sprang to Daliah's eyes as she tried to release all of her fear and doubt as she stood and hugged Olive. "I don't know what I would have

at the lightning sky. "Bet we'll make good time," he said, grinning when he realized that Spencer wasn't paying any attention at all.

***

The wagons rolled out across the prairie in a familiar train as the sun climbed halfway over the low horizon in shades of pink and purple and gray.

Deep shadows filled the valleys, but the long grass and sparse wildflowers reached for the sun's rays waving in reflected golds and greens, like a sea at sunset.

Spencer trotted to the head of the train, waving the others forward as he faced a new day. Barring any other catastrophes, they would reach his brother's town in a few more days. For the first time in years, he faced the new day with more in sight than the work of the day.

"God, I'm sorry I've been such a stubborn fool," Spencer said, gazing out across the sunbathed land. "I was angry and hurt, but you didn't let me get away and with your gentle hand, you've brought me hope. Thank you," he finished kicking his horse into an easy walk.

By nightfall, the travelers were busy discussing their plans for when they finally reached the no-name town. Several were continuing on to other locations, but more than half of the travelers had determined to stop in the town and see what they could make of it.

Mrs. Script's husband had been working for a trader in sales, and she had hopes of establishing a real store where people could get what they needed for their homesteads.

If rumors of a railroad to Texas were true, in only a few years, the town could be something completely new, and anyone established before then had the potential of making a good living as the town grew.

Several single men planned to sign on with cattle outfits, hunting parties, or building groups. Still, others had their hearts set on a piece of rich northern Texas soil where they could at the very least eke out a living off of the land.

Farmers, cattlemen, traders, and shopkeepers had all come together to start fresh in a new place. For many, it was what they needed most; a new start.

Daliah stepped up to Spencer as they sat around the fire. "What else did your brother tell you about the town?" she asked as she tried to picture the place.

She knew it was a new place that hadn't even been named yet but couldn't picture what the site was like. Would it be like the town they had left in Missouri with buildings lining a dusty street, or would it be simple huts and shacks cobbled together from whatever was available?

"He never said much," Spencer admitted sipping his coffee as others gathered around. "Dan wrote that the land was good and that he had staked out a good piece of land with some friends." Spencer paused, looking at the eager eyes all staring at him.

"Dan said after that a trader moved in on a crossroads and set up a trading post. Things are still rough, but a few other businesses are trying to make a go of it?"

"Have they built anything yet?" Mrs. Script asked. "My William is working for the trader but wants to start a proper store."

"I don't really know what kind of structures there are," Spencer admitted. "I told you every-thing I knew when you signed on."

People nodded, thinking back to his invitation months ago.

"Well, whatever it is, it'll be better than living out of our wagons," one of the single men spoke up.

"And maybe we can get a few head of good riding stock," another man said.

"I'm hoping Dan Gaines can use another hand," another man said.

"I don't know what I'm hoping for," old Ben spoke up, "but I think the fact that we can be part of something new is enough for me. In a few more days, we'll be there, and we'll see what's needed. It's a new start for many of us, and we'll make of it what we can," he finished rising and tossing the dregs of his coffee away before heading back to his wagon.

As others finished their dinner and began preparing for bed, Spencer took Daliah's hand and led her out under the stars for a walk.

"What do you hope for?" Spencer asked as they looked up at a half-moon. "Do you have your heart set on anything special?"

Daliah looked up into the heavens and thought about the question. "I don't know," she finally admitted. "All I know is that I needed a new start, and this is it. I'll be happy to work toward whatever you want," she finished, liking the way his hand felt wrapped around hers.

Spencer squeezed her hand. "Why did you leave Smithfield?" he asked gently. "I've heard rumors, but they don't fit the woman I've come to know."

Daliah lowered her eyes, her heart heavy that he had asked but realizing it was time she explained.

"I was accused of stealing money at the bank where I worked," Daliah said. "I didn't," she added quickly. "My drawer was counted out every night and balanced before I handed it off to the bank manager."

Spencer looked down at the small hand in his and nodded. "That's what I heard," he admitted. "I don't think anyone who knows you would ever believe it, though."

Daliah looked up into Spencer's face. "You believe me?"

"Of course I do," Spencer said. "Anyone in their right mind can see you aren't the type to take what isn't yours." He leaned down, kissing her gently and feeling the jolt of the kiss to his toes. Daliah would make his new life so much better.

"I'd better head back to the fire," Spencer finally said, breaking the kiss. "I need to get Chad to bed and check the camp."

Daliah nodded, relieved that he believed her story. However, the weight of the accusation was still painful even after this long, and she wanted to start their life together with no secrets.

Together they walked back to the camp, and Daliah somehow felt lighter, as if she no longer had to bear life's burdens alone.

"Daliah, will you put me to bed?" Chad called, walking up to them, knowing that there was no way to delay the inevitable.

"I'd love to," Daliah replied, taking the boy's hand, still holding to Spencer's as together they walked to the wagon they shared with Ben.

Daliah tucked Chad into his little spot at the wagon's tailgate, kissing his forehead as she settled him for sleep. "Now say your prayers," she said, sitting back on the tailgate.

"My prayers?" the boy asked. "Why?"

Spencer shuffled his feet in the dust of the prairie as guilt wriggled through his chest. "I'm afraid I've neglected such things," he said, looking at his son, "but this is a new start for all of us and if Daliah will help, I think we can all start saying our prayers again." Was it any wonder the boy had been in trouble so much?

Chad nodded, closing his eyes and folding his hands as Daliah bowed her head.

"Now I lay me down to sleep," she began, not noticing when Chad's eyes flew open again. "I pray the Lord my soul to keep,"

"I know this," Chad said interrupting, and then closing his eyes once more as Daliah and Spencer looked on. "Auntie Beth taught me."

"Would you like to continue?" Daliah asked, smiling at the boy.

"If I should die before I wake, I pray the Lord my soul to take," the boy finished. "Oh, and God bless us, everyone," he added, rolling over and snuggling into his blankets.

Chapter 18

Daliah looked up from where she sat next to Molly as Mr. Hampton pulled his horses to a stop at the edge of the town they had all been looking forward to for so long.

A tiny gasp escaped her lips as she gazed out across the mismatched tents and rubble-built shacks that dotted the flat top of the hill.

"Not exactly what you were picturing, is it?" Mrs. Hampton said, shaking her head.

In the distance, they could see one building that appeared to be made of wood and stone, but everything else was a mash-up of dwellings.

"I don't know what I was expecting," Daliah admitted. "I just hope I can be useful here in some way,"

Leaning to the side to get a better view of the town, Daliah spotted Spencer climbing down from his horse as another dark-haired man hurried to meet him at the edge of the town. When the men embraced, she smiled, realizing that the other man must be his brother.

"Whoa," Mr. Hampton said, pulling his horses to a stop. "We'll just wait here a spell until Spence tells us where we should lite."

A scream further up the wagon train made everyone turn to see Mrs. Script leap from the wagon into the outstretched arms of a stocky man with a shock of red hair and a beard.

Daliah smiled, reaching up to help Mrs. Hampton from the wagon. "I think this is going to be a good place," she said, her eyes twinkling with cheer.

"It just needs a little time and a few more women," Mrs. Hampton said.

"Dan, I'd like you to meet Ms. Owens and the Hamptons," Spencer said, hurrying down the street toward them. Reaching out, he took Daliah's arm, turning her toward his brother. "Daliah, this is my brother Dan."

"Pleased to meet you," Daliah said with a smile. She could see the resemblance between the brothers at a glance.

"Welcome," Dan said, shaking hands all around. "I'm mighty pleased to meet all of you. I hope you'll feel welcome here," he gestured around him. "For now, I'd like you to settle at the ranch until you figure out where you want to be."

"That sounds fine," Mr. Hampton said. "I can see there's work to be done at this here town."

"I'm afraid it isn't much of a town just yet," Dan admitted. "Tonight, we're all meeting at the saloon to discuss plans for all you folks," he added, pointing to the wooden building at the end of the street.

Daliah looked at Spencer, somewhat concerned as Chad came racing up, followed by Ben. "Pa, Pa is this our new home?" the boy asked.

"It sure is, son," Spencer said, grabbing his boy and lifting him up. "I'd like you to meet your uncle Dan as well," he added, turning to boy toward his brother.

"Hiya," Chad said, extending his hand and making Dan smile. "Is this where you live? It don't have any houses."

Dan chuckled. "I'm afraid this town is very new and in need of many things," Dan agreed, "but now that you are all here, we'll make it into something good."

***

The wagon train members dispersed to different areas setting up camps or sorting through possessions in preparation for starting their new home.

As the sun reached the edge of the western horizon, the whole town began to make their way to the saloon.

Dan Gaines stayed in town for the day and made the rounds, ensuring that everyone who could attend the big meeting would be there.

"You're rather an important man in this town," Spencer teased his younger brother as they walked through the open doors of the Saloon, Daliah on his arm.

"I was one of the first people to homestead, so people kind of look to me when anything new is happening."

Dan left Spencer and the small group of people with him and stepped up to the bar hooking his heel on the rail to give himself more height. The saloon was closed to serving anything but coffee for the night in deference to the woman and children, and as Dan called out, the gaggle of voices hushed.

"Well folks, it looks like things in this here place are about to change," he called, garnering a trickle of laughter from the rough-looking men that took up one side of the saloon.

"About time," one scruffy-looking individual with a bushy beard called out, "I'm tired of sleepin' under canvas."

Dan chuckled, waving the man to silence as others laughed, slapping each other on the back. "That's why I asked my brother to see if he could organize a wagon train to come to our humble town to help us flesh out some of the things we need."

"Need," another man called, "seems like there ain't nothin' we don't need."

"All right, you rogues settle down," Dan called. "Tonight, we're here to meet the new neighbors. First, I'd like to introduce my brother Spencer," Dan continued slapping his brother on the back. "Spence, if you'd introduce yourself and then have the folks that traveled with you introduce themselves as well. It'd be good to know what folks are looking for and what they're bringing to our town."

Spencer stood his hat in his hands as he gazed out over the crowd. "Hello," he started. "I'm Spencer Gaines, Dan's big brother, and I've come down here to make sure he doesn't get into too much trouble." The laughter that met that remark rattled the windows, but soon the men settled down again. "I had a little ranch a few years back, but when my wife died, I got restless. So I'm hoping to make this a real home for my son and me," he said, waving at Chad, who waved back from his seat next to Daliah. "This young lady is Daliah Owens, who has consented to marry me as soon as we can find a preacher," he finished noting how some of the other men seemed to grumble at the statement.

Daliah looked up prettily, blushing slightly at

the attention, but Spencer's bright smile and twinkling eyes made her feel loved.

"The folks with her are the Hamptons. Mr. Hampton, if you'd introduce yourself," He finished stepping aside as the older man stood.

"I'm Orville Hampton," the old man said, "and I'm an old sawyer. Some of these hills here about are full of good trees, and I'd like to start a mill so's folks can start building good sturdy housing that will last. My wife Olive and me are looking forward to seeing what we can do for this town."

Several men clapped as one shouted out. "We have been needin' a mill. I won't complain about four walls around me."

"We need a mill." Someone else called.

"We need a store too," another voice called.

"And a livery!" another shouted.

"Seems to me this is a mighty needful town," Mrs. Hampton said loudly to her husband just as the noise quieted.

A heavy hush fell over the meeting place and only the creak of a chair or the scuff of a boot could be heard.

"Needful, hey?" Dan said, looking at Mrs. Hampton, whose face was tinted with embarrassment. "Needful. I reckon that pretty much sums it up," he continued. "What do y'all think about that?" he

DALIAH

asked. "Needful, Texas sounds about right to me."

Spencer stepped up to Daliah taking her hand as a hushed conversation ensued, gazing into her eyes as his thumb drew little circles on the back of her hand and sheltering her protectively.

"Looks like your brother needs a preacher," the man with the bushy beard called with a hearty laugh.

"You mind your manners, Greg," Dan chided as others laughed.

"Needful sounds good to me," one of the wranglers said. "We need a good many things."

"Is everyone agreed?" Dan called, waving the men down. "All in favor of finally naming this forsaken patch of earth. Needful raise your hand and say, aye."

Every hand in the place seemed to raise and the resounding ayes echoed through the room.

"Anyone not in favor?" Dan called one more time but was met with silence. "Well, let's get back to introductions then..."

"Help! Help!" a woman's voice called as a short black-haired woman with dark skin rushed into the saloon. "I need doctor, please. Is there a doctor?"

Dan hurried to the woman taking her hands in his as he tried to calm her. "We don't have a doctor," he said. "What's wrong? What has happened?"

The woman collapsed into tears as Dan tried to comfort her.

"My bambino, my bambino," she sobbed.

"Dan, Daliah's mighty good with fixin' people up," Spencer said, joining his brother with Daliah in tow.

"Please help," the other woman cried, grasping Daliah by the arm.

"I'll help," Daliah said. "Please take me to your baby."

Together the small group hurried out the door, Daliah casting a knowing glance back at Mrs. Hampton, who gathered Chad to her.

"Spencer, will you fetch my bag, please? It's in the wagon," Daliah said, practically running to keep up with the smaller woman.

In a few moments, Dan, Daliah, and the woman were ducking into the drafty tent with a small cot and what appeared to be a bundle of rags in a basket.

Daliah leaned over the bundle and peered in at the tiny baby who was gurgling and struggling for breath. "Boil water," she said, her voice snapping as she lifted the little thing from the basket.

The other woman jumped to comply, grabbing a bucket and kicking a fire pit back to life under a large black kettle at the front of the tent.

"Daliah?" Spencer said, walking in, a lamp in one hand and her bag in another.

"Here," Daliah replied, handing the baby off to Spencer as she took the bag, rummaging for what she needed until she pulled out a vile of pungent-smelling liquid.

"Unwrap her," Daliah said, spilling a drop of the liquid onto her finger and rubbing it on the baby's chest.

Spencer blinked as the strong smell of menthol, eucalyptus, and something else assailed his nostrils.

"The water's almost boiling," Dan said, ducking his head back into the tent. "Rosa, the mother, has been here a couple of weeks cooking for some of the men in town."

Daliah nodded. "Dan could you go and ask Mrs. Hampton to get some tea on," she said, taking the baby back from Spencer. "Spencer, I need a basin for the water." Together the men stepped out into the darkness, disappearing.

"Rosa," Daliah called and the other woman stepped inside, wringing her hands. "What brought you to Needful?" Daliah asked, trying to calm the woman and using the town's new name for the first time.

"My husband, he is working on a drive. He brings cattle to New Mexico. I cannot stay alone, so I come here."

"Will this do?" Spencer stepped back into the softly lit tent with a basin. Daliah nodded, handing the baby to its mother and hurrying back to the kettle. In a few moments, she had the basin filled with hot water as she dripped more of the aromatic liquid into the water then held the baby over the steam, keeping her hand close to its face to make sure the baby didn't get too warm.

Rosa stood beside her, wringing her hands with fear.

"Daliah, I brought tea," Mrs. Hampton said, stepping into the tent with Dan on her heels. "You men clear off now," the older woman said, waving at Dan and Spencer. "We'll call you if you're needed."

Spencer smiled for what felt like the first time in hours as the baby gagged and choked.

Olive handed Rosa a cup of tea. "You drink this, dear," she said. "Daliah will do all she can."

Again the baby hacked, coughing from deep in her lungs as the congestion broke and the baby retched up the choking phlegm.

"That's better," Daliah said, breathing for the

first time as she dipped a rag in cool water and washed the baby's face, grinning at its soft cry.

"Thank you, thank you," Rosa said, fresh tears pouring down her face as Daliah handed the baby back to her.

"If she gets bad again, you will need to do this again," Daliah said. "For now, keep this cloth on her chest," she said, dabbing more of the potent liquid onto a rag. "It will help keep her airways open."

Rosa tucked the still crying child into her arm and reached out to hug Daliah. "Gracious Dios," the woman said. "God brought you when we needed you."

Daliah suddenly felt exhausted and Olive pulled her and Rosa down to sit on the cot, pressing cups into their hands once more.

"Seems to me that this town needs a decent restaurant," the older woman said, lifting the teapot and another cup for herself. "I think I'll be talking to Orville about that first thing."

Daliah smiled, seeing the older woman's mind whirling away with plans.

"This is Christina," Rosa said, lifting the now quieted baby. "She is our first bambino."

Daliah looked down at the baby's puckered face and smiled as she blinked back at her. "Raoul and me, we work hard. We come to this part of Texas to make a better life, but now he goes away, and I must stay."

"Well, you aren't alone no more," Olive said. "Once me and Orville get things goin', you'll come and work with us, and I tell you, we'll do some good around here. With Daliah here getting' married, I'll need someone to help me if you'll agree."

Rosa nodded. "I would like that, Seniora," she said. "Thank you."

Chapter 19

Three long weeks of hard work and toil passed, but Daliah looked out over the town with loving eyes. She was still staying with the Hamptons as she and Spencer waited for a traveling preacher to arrive.

She couldn't believe what had transpired in the three weeks since the wagon train had come to a stop in Needful.

The trading post was busier than ever but couldn't accommodate the growing town, and Mr. Script had taken his wagon and hired another one as he and Trey set out east toward the river where they could buy supplies for the general store they were planning.

Mr. Hampton had wrangled some of the younger men and headed for the hills to mark and cut trees that would be hand split to build new homes and businesses. He had brought one of the older blades from the mill in Smithfield and was looking forward to starting work on the sawmill that was so badly needed.

It was a busy time but full of friendship, hope, and goodwill, even with the occasional drunken cowboy racing his horse through town.

Almost immediately after she and the Hamptons had set up their meager living accommodations outside Dan's property, people had started coming to Daliah for minor injuries and medical assistance. She had been overwhelmed at the number of cuts, abrasions, and bellyaches she'd dealt with in rapid order.

"You're as close as this place comes to a doctor," Spencer said one evening when he came to call. "You have to expect people coming to you for help."

"Just as long as no one expects me to pull a tooth," Daliah said with a shiver. "I draw the line at that,"

Spencer chuckled, squeezing her hand in his. "One of the riders said he thought a preacher might be through soon," the one-time trail boss said with a grin. "Will you be ready to marry me when he gets here?'

Daliah turned to the man whom she was falling in love with, a little more each day. "I think I will," she said with some pluck. "I don't know what you want me for, but I'll be glad to be yours," she added with a grin.

Spencer spun her toward him, pulling her into

his arms and looking down at her. "I want you for so many things in my life," he said thoughtfully. "You help me be a better man. You challenge me to remember that with the bad comes something good and that God has a purpose for us on this dusty patch of earth. You're good, and kind, and loving," he finished lowering his lips to her and reminding her that God's word said it was not good for a man to be alone.

Daliah reeled back from the kiss, her head spinning with the passion that coursed through her. She had never even had a beau before, and this man did delightful things to her sensibilities. Yes, she would most definitely be ready to marry Spencer when the preacher arrived.

Spencer stepped away from Daliah, pulling himself back together. He didn't deserve this caring young woman who already loved his son like her own, but he would do his best to be the best husband he could be.

He couldn't count the number of times she'd kept the boy out of one scrape or another on the trail, and the way she had been willing to put herself in danger for Chad had eroded the excuses he had made to guard his heart. No, he was ready for that preacher to get there soon, and in the meantime, he would work hard to build a place on his brother's land that they could move into.

Most days, Spencer worked young horses for his

brother in the morning then headed to town to help with laying out the building that Olive Hampton was determined to have. At least if they did have to wait longer than he liked to marry, he could make sure that Daliah and the older couple would have a decent roof overhead before winter.

"Querido Cielo," Rosa said, walking into the portion of the log structure that the Hamptons had started. "It is very big," she added, adjusting a sparkling-eyed Christina on her hip.

"It will be our home and our business," Olive said. "This is the kitchen at the back, then a small shop to sell bread and baked goods, and finally an eating area here. For this winter, we'll use part of the back for our quarters and put a roof up, and then next spring, add another floor. You and Christina will stay here," she finished indicating a room of about ten feet square.

"This is not necessary," Rosa said.

"I'll be mighty glad to have you," Olive said. "With Daliah marrying Spencer, I'll need the help," she added with a smile and when Raoul returns, he can stay here until you have a place of your own."

Rosa smiled. "Dios de bendiga," Rosa said.

"I come to help out," a craggy voice called from outside the structure. "Orville said you was cookin' for anyone what would come and pitch in with the work," the man finished.

Olive smiled, winking at Rosa. "Yes, we are," she said. "I'll show you what to do."

Another two weeks ticked by and Daliah was kept busy, cooking, helping with minor medical issues, and spending time with Spencer and Chad.

Dan and Orville seemed to have a way of motivating the men working in the area, to improve the town. Several times the men had meetings in the saloon and Daliah would laugh every time Orville and Spencer came home to Olive, pestering them about what was said.

The older woman was a force of her own, working behind the scenes to see that the town would grow into something lasting.

"What we need is more women," Olive said to Daliah one afternoon as they sat in their tent sipping tea. "There are far too many single men and not enough women. Why just last night, there was a drunken brawl down at the saloon."

Daliah smiled, wondering what the woman was planning but biding her time. Soon she would be a married woman herself, and she could be patient if she had to. Sooner or later, whatever Olive Hampton had in her head would come out.

A bright afternoon sun beat down on the town of Needful as a lone horseman in a black frock coat road into town, ambling his horse along the crooked main street and scanning the industrious building projects.

Daliah peered at the man curiously from her place in the newly framed window hole of the Hampton House, her heart fluttering in anticipation. Surely he was the preacher they had been waiting for.

Curious eyes peered out at the stranger as men stopped their work to watch him ride by.

"Howdy stranger," Orville called as the man pulled up near a grove of fat oaks near a cool spring. "What can we do for you?"

"I'm Pastor Jay," the man said, looking down at Orville. "I see you folks are mighty busy here. Do you think you'll have time for services on Sunday?"

"I think you'd better step down a spell," Orville said with a smile. "We'd be mighty pleased to have you stay a spell. I know some folks been waiting for you."

***

Daliah fidgeted as Olive adjusted the buttons on the pretty gold and blue gown.

"Would you settle down?" Olive chided. "Tomorrow's soon enough to be nervous."

"I'm sorry," Daliah said. She'd been a bundle

of nerves and excitement ever since Spencer had talked to the preacher. Olive had insisted that they alter Daliah's mother's dress, only adding to the jittery feeling roiling in Daliah's stomach. Tomorrow after the Sunday service, she would become Daliah Gaines, and she couldn't help but feel that something was going to happen to steal her joy.

"You're as nervous as a long-tailed cat in a room full of rockers," Olive said, unbuttoning the dress. "Aren't you sure about Spence and Chad?"

"Oh my yes!" Daliah cried. "I've never been more sure of anything in my life. I love Spencer and Chad is the light of my life."

A heavy knock landed on the door, making Olive look up as she helped Daliah out of the fancy dress and into her simple daily wear.

Outside the room, she could hear Orville greeting someone and she hurried to hang the dress up while Daliah finished changing.

The men of the town had worked overtime to finish the Hampton House and restaurant and to her great surprise, the outer structure of the upstairs and roof was already on. Of course, there was plenty of work inside yet to be done, but it was coming along and the kitchen and dining area were functional.

Already the preacher was taking up a spot on the bare floor above. She knew that the eatery would be busier than ever.

"I'll just step out and see who that is," Olive said, slipping through the door and closing it behind her.

Outside Daliah caught the rumble of Spencer's voice and hurried to get ready so that they could share supper together.

"Hello," she called cheerfully, stepping out of the small room then looking up in concern at all of the people staring back at her. "What's wrong?" Daliah asked, her hands shaking as she took in Mr. Scripts, holding a rolled paper and standing by the door. "Is Chad all right?" she asked, her voice cracking.

"Daliah, I think you need to sit down," Orville said, taking her arm and leading her to a chair.

"Why? What's going on?" Daliah asked, fear turning her stomach to acid.

"I'm telling you...." Spencer hissed to Mr. Scripts, "there has to be a mistake."

"What's going on?" Daliah demanded.

"Miss Owens?" Mr. Scripts' eyes were sad, "I'm sorry about this," he said, smoothing his neatly trimmed beard. "When we went for supplies, we found this at the sheriff's office," he finished apologetically unfurling the paper before her.

Daliah felt the blood drain from her face as the image on the page swam before her eyes, and her head spun as the world faded to black.

She never even felt Spencer's strong arms capture her before she slipped to the hard floor, nor did she feel his hot tears falling on her cold, pale cheeks.

Chapter 20

"This isn't right," Spencer's loud voice was the first thing that Daliah heard as her eyes fluttered open and the world came back into existence.

"What happened?" Daliah whispered, trying to rise from the floor.

"You fainted, dear," Mrs. Hampton said, patting her hand.

Daliah struggled to rise and Spencer was at her side, instantly helping her to the chair she had fallen from minutes ago, while Orville pressed a cup of water into her hand.

"Spencer, what's going on?" Daliah asked, rubbing her temple with one hand while she clung to his with the other.

Spencer squeezed her hand, looking toward Mr. Scripts, who still stood in the middle of the room, looking worried and upset.

"Oh," Daliah sighed, dropping her head in her hands as sobs took her breath away.

"It's all right, honey," Spencer said, his hands protectively resting on her shoulders.

"Don't worry. You didn't do anything, and we'll prove it."

Daliah shook her head dejectedly. Her life had finally taken a turn for the best and her heart had been so full of hope. She was going to be a wife and little Chad would be her new son, but now it was all shattered and scattered on the dry earth like broken pottery.

"It's no use," Daliah hiccupped. "No one will believe me. I'm just a nobody orphan. As long as this is hanging over my head, I can't marry you," she finished, her eyes swimming.

Spencer moved around to the front of the chair, his hands holding tight to her shoulders as he squatted before her. "It will be all right," he repeated, begging her to look him in the eyes. "Look at me, Daliah," he said, her name on his lips making her meet his troubled gaze. "I promise everything will work out."

Daliah looked into Spencer's earnest face wanting to believe him. She thought she had escaped this when she left Smithfield. She hadn't been charged with a crime. She hadn't even been publicly shamed. So why had it caught up to her now?

"I don't know what is going on here," Daliah said, rising to her feet, "but I did not steal anything from the bank." Then, taking a short turn around the room, she circled back to Spencer. "As long as this is hanging over my head, I won't marry you, Spencer Gaines. I won't bring that kind of a shame to your family."

Spencer wrapped an arm around her, pulling her close and offering his support. Behind her, she could hear Mr. and Mrs. Hampton stepping close. Her family was behind her.

"It doesn't matter to me," Spencer insisted. "I know your heart and I know you would never do anything like this. We can still get married tomorrow, then work this out."

Daliah shook her head, unable to believe that everything would be fine.

"Spence, I think the sheriff will be along eventually asking questions or worse, maybe some bounty hunters," Mr. Script said. "I thought you should know," he added, twisting his battered hat in his hands.

"Daliah just got here," Spencer said, looking up at William Scripts, his eyes hard. "I can't believe this is happening." He turned, looking at the woman who had quietly stolen his heart, and shook his head. "No one is coming to take you away," he said. "You're needed here. People need you. I need you." He pulled her close, wrapping his arms around her protectively. "I'm going to fix this."

Daliah pulled back slowly, fear making her heart race. "How?" she asked, worried about what Spencer might do.

"I'm going back to Smithfield to clear your name once and for all."

Daliah shook her head slowly, shock overwhelming her. Spencer was leaving her. Just like everyone else she had ever loved.

"I'll be back honey," Spencer's words were earnest as he placed his hands on either side of her face. "I promise," he continued reaching down and taking her hands in his before kissing her fingers. "I'll be back."

***

"Spencer!" Daliah called, rushing out onto the newly covered porch of the tall structure the following day as Spencer led his horse to the door. "Please don't do this?" she begged. "I'll go back. You're needed here. What about Chad?" she added, falling into Spencer's arms as Olive and Orville walked out with the boy.

"Why are you going, Pa?" Chad asked, his eyes filling with tears. "I thought this was gonna be our home?"

Spencer squatted down, pulling Chad close and holding him for a long minute before replying.

"This is our home," he said, leaning back and looking into his son's face. "But sometimes a man has to stand up and do the right thing to protect the ones he loves. You'll be all right here with Daliah and the Hamptons, just like before when I had to take to the trails."

"But I don't want you to go," Chad sniffed. "I want you to stay here and marry Daliah and eat brown sugar dumplings every night."

Spencer pulled the boy in close one more time. "I'll be back," he said. "I'll be back, and we'll marry Daliah once this is all set straight. I know what to do," he added, standing and looking into the faces of people who had become so much more than friends. "You promise to mind Daliah and do what she says while I'm gone," he finished.

"I will, Pa," Chad agreed, rubbing the tears from his eyes, "and I'll say my prayers every night, so's God will take care of you till you're home again."

Spencer choked back the lump in his throat, lifting the boy in his arm and pulling Daliah in for a group hug. "I love you both," he said. "I'll be back when this is finished."

Handing Chad to Daliah, he turned away, climbing into the saddle and riding down the street.

Chapter 21

Daliah watched the man she loved turn away, holding tight to Chad's hand, as Spencer rode out of sight.

"He'll be back, won't he?" The boy asked, his damp eyes imploring.

Daliah squatted in the dust of the street, placing her hands on Chad's shoulders and meeting his gaze. "He'll be back," she said, feeling a strange sense of peace settle into her heavy heart. "We'll pray for him every day," she added, lifting her eyes to God in silent supplication. Her heart still ached for Spencer to turn around and ride back to her, but she knew one way or another he would be home again, and she would be right there waiting for him.

Chad folded his hands and bowed his head as the sun cast its warm rays across the town. "God, Daliah says you love everyone, and you see everything, so if you would, please watch over my pa and bring him home soon. Amen."

Daliah felt the tears rolling down her cheeks

again as she pulled the boy into her arms and into her heart.

"Good morning," a jarringly cheerful voice said, making them all look up. "I thought we were having a wedding here today," the preacher said, pulling a shiny gold watch from his pocket and examining it.

"I'm afraid the wedding will have to wait," Daliah said, rising and taking Chad's hand. "Mr. Gaines had to leave suddenly," she said, her voice breaking in near despair.

Mrs. Hampton hurried out of the house, wrapping an arm around Daliah's shoulders and looked at the man expectantly.

"I'm sorry to hear that," the preacher said, tucking his watch back into his pocket and shaking his head. "Let us pray for his safety and success."

***

Spencer looked out across the grass of the prairie along the trail he had traveled so recently and forced himself not to look back.

"This surely isn't fair," Spencer spoke to his sturdy bay gelding as they trotted across the open ground. "Daliah doesn't need to be a part of this anymore. She didn't do anything and one way or another I'm going to prove it."

He kicked the horse into a ground-eating gallop.

After a quarter-mile, Spencer let the horse slow again as his mind turned the problem over again in his mind. It wouldn't be easy finding the person who had blamed Daliah for their crimes. He wasn't going to be able to ride into town and point the finger at the miscreant.

No, this would require some serious thought and a good deal of effort. Spencer's heart constricted in his chest as he thought of the long ride and ever-growing miles between him and his family. Perhaps Daliah had balked at going through with the wedding after this mess, but to him, she was his heart and nothing would change that.

"Seems like me and Daliah have suffered enough already," Spencer's rich voice made his horse's ears twitch. "You'd think we could catch a break about now."

Leaning over, he patted the horse's neck with a sigh. "We'll just have to do our best," he said. "Maybe we'll get a little help," he added as he lifted his eyes to a clear blue sky, his heart heavy as lead. "God, please," he pleaded. "You only just got through this thick head that I could love again. Don't let it be for nothing."

***

"Daliah," Rosa knocked on the door of the small room that had been added onto the Hampton House for Daliah and Chad in the weeks since Spencer had gone.

"Does someone need me?" Daliah asked, looking at the lovely petite woman with weary eyes.

"No," Rosa said, "but someone wants to see you," she said, opening the door and letting one of the young men from the original wagon train in.

"Miss Owens," the man said as he twisted his hat in his hands.

"Hello, Jack," Daliah said listlessly. Since Spencer's departure, she felt like she was going through the motions of living, but she pasted a smile on her face for the sake of others.

"Miss Owens, I was mighty sorry to hear about Spencer," the young man said, swallowing hard to stifle his nervousness. "I only just heard a few days ago when we brought a herd in from Mexico."

"Thank you, Jack," Daliah said. People in town had been very kind to her since the wanted poster had been found and Spencer left. The people from the wagon train assured her that they didn't believe any of the nonsense they had heard and that they stood behind her. But, still, she cried herself to sleep almost every night, longing for Spencer to return.

"The thing is," Jack continued. "I remember when that all happened," he said, nearly crushing his hat brim. "I got to thinkin' ya see. One day, I was at the bank takin' out some money to get ready for this trip, and I saw Mr. Shaw puttin' money in his pocket. I never did think anything of it since he was the bank manager. So I figured he was taking funds to use for the bank or some such thing," Jack finished looking at her pale face.

Daliah stood, her hands shaking as she stepped toward Jack. "You're sure?" she asked, taking his arms and looking into his eyes.

"Yes, ma'am," he said. "I told Dan, and he wrote it out, and I signed my mark to it then lit out for Dallas with his best string of horses. He told me to come and let you know. Said he'd mail this to Smithfield and hope it helped. I reckon he'll be back in a few days the way he was riding."

Bright tears filled Daliah's eyes and she squeezed the man's arms with one hand as if he might slip away if she let go. "Come with me," she said, turning and pulling him out of the room.

"Daliah, what's wrong?" Mrs. Hampton said as the door opened and the young woman stepped through the young wrangler in tow.

"Tell her," Daliah said, her voice breaking as a smile settled over her face.

"Alabad a Dios," Rosa said from where she stood

by the stove stirring a pot, her little girl cooing at her from a basket on the floor when Jack finished his story.

"Did someone say something about Pa?" Chad asked, hurrying into the house with Mr. Hampton, his arms full of kindling.

"We have a witness that knows who stole the money from the bank," Olive said, looking at Orville.

"Does that mean Pa can come home?" Chad asked, looking between the adults in hope and confusion.

"I think it does," Daliah breathed.

Chapter 22

Spencer walked into the Marshall's office in Smithfield, trail weary and dry as dust. His hard eyes glinted at the older man sitting behind a big desk when he stepped up, removing his hat as his boots clicked on the solid floor.

"What can I do for you, young man?" the Marshall asked, squinting at him with dark, intelligent eyes that offset his beaky nose and heavy mustache.

Spencer studied the man for two heartbeats, wondering if the graying lawman had been the one to send those posters of Daliah to Texas.

"I'm here," he started clearing his dry throat, "I'm here about Daliah Owens."

"You don't say?" The Marshall shifted some of the papers on his desk, pulling one from the pile and turning it toward Spencer. "You here for the reward?"

"No sir," Spencer said, glaring down at the superficial likeness of the woman he loved. "I'm here to clear her name."

The Marshall rose slowly until he stood face to face with Spencer, looking him in the eye. "You saying she's innocent?" the Marshall asked, his gruff voice soft.

"I am," Spencer growled.

"And who are you when you're at home?" the Marshall asked, leaning forward slightly. "Why should I believe you?"

"I'm Spencer Gaines and I'm going to marry that girl," Spencer's words were clipped and he expected the older man to push back.

"You don't say?" The Marshall's bright smile made Spencer blink. "So you say she didn't do this thievin', do ya?"

"The woman I know would never take anything that wasn't hers. She's kind, loving, caring, and giving. She worked tirelessly to help others on the trail to Texas and even now, with this hanging over her head, is working to make Needful a home for my son and me."

"Whoa, whoa, son. No need to get riled. I've thought something smelled rotten about this whole thing ever since Mr. Shaw brought it to me." Moving to a small stove near the door, the Marshall took two cups down from a peg, filling them with coffee. "I'm Marshal Eagan," the man continued.

"Have a seat and we'll jaw a spell."

Spencer raised his brows, surprised at the lawman's words but took the cup gratefully before sinking into a chair as he listened to the Marshall explain what led to the wanted posters.

"So you're telling me a month after we left Smithfield for Texas, Mr. Shaw found discrepancies in the bank's books and came to you to file charges against a young woman who had been dismissed three weeks earlier?" Spencer asked, incredulously, a half-hour later.

"Yep, that about sums it up," Tom Eagan said, smoothing his mustache thoughtfully. "He figured she had been taking a little bit at a time so people wouldn't notice until she was gone."

"That makes no sense at all," Spencer said, placing his mug on the desk and rising to pace the small room. "How much was missing?" he finally asked, wheeling and looking the Marshall in the eye.

"Nearly three-hundred dollars," the other man said.

"If she had been taking a few dollars a week, it would have taken months to steal that much and there is no way that the manager or the president or one of the other clerks wouldn't have noticed."

"That's pretty much what I thought," Marshall

Eagan agreed. "But when I checked up on everyone, I couldn't find anything to prove it."

Again Spencer took a turn around the small room, glancing out the window on his final pass. "I'll find it," he said, turning and slamming his palms onto the desk. "I'll prove that Daliah didn't do it!"

"Now we're talkin'," Marshall Eagan said, planting his palms on the other side of the desk and rising to stare at Spencer across the desk. "You'll need this," he finished reaching into his pocket and slapping a shiny badge on the desk. "Tell you what," the older man said, smoothing his bushy mustache. "You can be my unofficial deputy and keep house here while you dig. It's pretty quiet roundabout town but for this mess. The cots in the cells ain't uncomfortable, and you can save some coin at the same time you're clearin' your gal's name."

Spencer looked across the desk at the older man, studying him carefully before standing to his full height before reaching out a hand to shake on the arrangement.

***

Spencer Gaines bellied up to the bar in the local saloon and ordered a beer before turning to the bartender and hitching a heel over the rail.

Pushing his hat back on his head, he gazed out

across the tables spread across the room where men were gambling. He had taken his time moving along the street after the bank closed but had followed Mr. Shaw to the establishment a short time ago and now he watched as the little man wiped a handkerchief across his damp forehead, then lifted his hand.

In just the few minutes that Spencer stood there watching, he could see that the man was a poor gambler. He risked too much and couldn't bluff well enough to fool a four-year-old.

As the game progressed in the hot, smoke-filled room, Spencer watched the twitchy little man bet more and more only to lose it in one hand after another. Tallying the amount of each bet quickly in his head, it became apparent to Spencer that Mr. Shaw seemed to have a good deal more money than any bank manager would earn in a year, let alone a month. Just how was he funding his game of chance?

Turning back to the bar, Spencer examined his face in the mirror. His blue eyes were hard and he could feel the urge to go to the table, grab Mr. Shaw by the coat and drag him to the Marshall building in his chest. If anyone was guilty of embezzlement and thievery, Mr. Shaw fit the bill down to his toes, but right now, that wouldn't help Daliah. He needed proof. So instead, swirling the amber liquid in his cup, Spencer continued to study Mr. Shaw, watching each movement and reading each pathetic tell.

***

"I'm telling you, Tom," Spencer said, after nearly a week of following Mr. Shaw and observing his bad habits, "Mr. Shaw is the only one who could have taken that money."

For the past week, Marshall Eagan had let Spencer stay in the jail and keep an eye on things while trying to prove that Daliah couldn't have stolen money from the Smithfield Bank.

"First," he started again, ticking points off his calloused fingers. "he gambles at least twice a week and always loses. Second, he can't possibly earn as much as he is losing, and third, he has I-owe-you's out to at least three town toughs."

"That doesn't prove anything," Marshall Eagan said. "A man can have debt, be a bad gambler, and an all-around rotten character and still not be a thief. You have to have proof."

Spencer pinched the bridge of his nose, letting the air out of his lungs with a whoosh. "What do I have to find?" he asked. "How do I prove it? He is the only one who could have taken the money. He has access to all of the tills and the safe. He also helps keep the books so that when something goes a miss, he can rewrite the books to cover his tracks."

"If it's so easy to cook the books, why would he need to go blamin' your girl for stealing the money?" the Marshall asked, making Spencer steam.

"I don't know," Spence admitted, pulling a little notebook from his pocket. "When did he make the accusation?" He flipped through the pages. "Here it is," he continued. "It was just over three weeks after Daliah left with the wagon train. He took sick and was away from the bank for three days. When he got back, Mr. Bradford called him for a meeting. It was after that he came here and filed the charges against Daliah. According to Mr. Bradford, there was a transaction that didn't add up when he had balanced the week's receipts."

Marshall Eagan smoothed his thick graying mustache. "It makes sense," he agreed. "I think I'll just have a chat with Mr. Bradford again," he finally said, standing and walking to the door where he took his hat from a peg and slapped it onto his head. "You coming?" he tossed over his shoulder with a grin.

***

Spencer crept into the empty house, listening for every sound. He had to find the proof that would clear Daliah's name and let her marry him when he returned to Needful. It had taken him a month and a half riding hard to get back to Smith-field, and now three weeks later, he still felt like he was no closer to solving this crime and giving Daliah that new start that they both wanted.

The dark house smelled musty. The old structure, small and run down at the outskirts of town, didn't seem fitting to a man of Mr. Shaw's means. That in itself was suspicious to Spencer.

After the meeting with the bank President, Spencer knew that if he didn't find some evidence soon, Daliah would never be free from this. Mr. Bradford had told them everything he knew but couldn't believe that his trusted manager would do anything wrong. The very fact that Daliah left town mere weeks before the discrepancies were found was damning enough in his eyes.

Spencer stubbed his toe on a rickety chair and hissed a breath through clenched teeth to stifle the pain, but still, he was no closer to finding anything. He dug through drawers around the small house, checked between books, and looked under furniture, but came up empty-handed.

As the minutes ticked by and he realized he wasn't going to find anything without a daylight search, Spencer crept out the back door and took a turn around the backyard. In the far corner of the overgrown space, a large bucket sat below a tree. A warm breeze ruffled the leaves of the old cottonwood stirring the ashes in the bucket and Spencer hurried forward to peer inside.

Several small, partially burned pages fluttered in the wind and Spencer pulled the pieces that were still intact carefully to him, trying to read them by the light of a half-moon.

Giving it up for a bad job, Spencer slipped the pages into a pocket and let himself out of an old misused gate. This was taking too long. Any day now, someone could find Daliah in Needful and she would know he had failed.

Making his way back to the jailhouse where he had taken up residence, Spencer lit a lamp then sat at the oversized desk flipping through the bits of paper. The numbers and markings made the hair on the back of his neck stand on end, and Spencer knew he had found his first actual proof.

***

"Spencer, you're coming with me," Marshall Eagan said, rattling the cell where Spencer spent every night. "You'll need this," the Marshal added, tossing the man a badge with a grin.

In the weeks he had been back in Smithfield, Spencer had worked tirelessly tracking down every lead he could to clear Daliah of any wrongdoing, but every night he would return to the jailhouse trying to put the pieces of information together that would let him go home.

He had talked to the bank president, shop keepers, and acquaintances. None of them could believe that Daliah was guilty of wrongdoing, but the circumstances surrounding the loss of the large sum of money and the conscience of Daliah leaving the wagon train along with her previous dismissal for missing funds had prompted the bank's owners to act.

"What's happening, Tom?" Spencer asked, pinning the badge to his coat and hurrying to catch up.

The old Marshall grinned, his mustache quivering over thin lips, as he shoved a telegram into Spencer's hands. "We're going to make an arrest," he said, pushing his ten-gallon hat onto his head and opening the door to the jail.

The raid happened in what seemed like seconds. Spencer and Tom swooped into the bank, hauling Mr. Shaw, the bank manager, from his tiny office.

"Unhand me!" the man barked as the Marshall took him by one arm and Spencer by the other. "You can't treat me like this!"

"Mr. Shaw, you are under arrest for embezzlement from the Smithfield bank and for trying to pin it on a young woman who wouldn't hurt a fly." Tom Eagan said roughly.

"It's a good thing the law got to you first," Spencer hissed at the little man whose forehead now glistened with beads of sweat. "You should be horsewhipped for what you did to Daliah."

"I didn't hurt no one," the man quivered with fear leaning closer to the Marshall. "What's that useless orphan to you anyhow?"

Spencer balled his fist and turned his eyes, blazing at the man with hard eyes. "Daliah Owens is a kind, gentle, and loving woman, and my fiancée," he hissed. "You practically ruined her for a fist full of dollars."

Mr. Shaw gulped, his eyes going as wide as saucers as he crowded closer to the Marshall while the town's people watched the procession down the street to the jailhouse with morbid curiosity.

By the time Mr. Shaw was safely locked away in the cell, the weasely little man had confessed to everything, cringing each time he looked at Spencer. As worried as he was about Spencer's anger, he seemed almost relieved to have been caught. At least behind bars, the men he owed money to wouldn't be able to get to him.

"Well, I'd say that about does it then," Marshall Eagan said with a grin as he closed the door to the room containing the cells. "Daliah's been cleared and won't need to serve time for a job you didn't do. I sent a few men over to Mr. Shaw's house to find the strongbox and recover what's left of the money," he added, with a shake his head. "Fool man, getting himself into that kind of debt gambling. I'll send out notices canceling the wanted posters too," he finished.

Spencer unpinned the badge from his coat and handed it toward the Marshall. "Thank you for believing me."

Tom Eagan chuckled. "I'm a sucker for a love story, I guess," he said. "You keep that," he added, nodding toward the badge. "I have a feeling it might come in useful on your trip home. You never know when you might need to sort out a mystery or wrangle someone back onto the straight and narrow."

The Marshall moved to a small stove in the corner of the office and filled two cups with coffee handing one to Spencer, who tucked the badge into his breast pocket.

"I don't understand," Spencer said, sipping the black brew.

"Son, you gathered more evidence in three weeks than I had in nearly three months. I didn't believe that girl could have pulled off that kind of stunt, you see. You don't think I didn't try before sending those posters out, do you? No, everything I found pointed to that worthless being sitting in my jail cell. I didn't have enough evidence to prove it until I got that telegram. You've got good instincts and, more importantly, a good heart. You'll be just what that new town needs as it grows."

Spencer raised a brow over his cup of coffee but didn't say anything. All he knew was that this mess was over and he could go home.

***

Spencer walked down the stairs of the small courthouse, a bright smile on his face as he headed for his horse and pack mules.

The trial had been short and sweet and the sentencing just. Mr. Shaw had confessed to everything. There was little else for him to do but beg for the mercy of the courts since he'd been caught with the bank's money in his own home. Yet, despite all the trouble the man had caused and the pain he had caused Spencer and those he loved, Spencer still offered a prayer for him as he reached the street.

"You ain't leavin' without saying goodbye, are you?" Marshall Eagan said, catching up and extending his hand.

Switching his reins to his other hand, Spencer clasped the Marshall's hand. "I'm headin' home," Spencer said. "Just as fast as I can."

"You have something nice to go home to," the Marshall said, clapping his other hand over Spencer's. "Looks like you're ready for a fast trip," he added, releasing the younger man and nodding toward the extra riding horse and the mules.

"I might set a record," Spencer said with a laugh. "I hope my brother gets my letter before I get there," he added. "I'd like him to know what happened."

"Pretty soon, you'll have the railroad coming your way there in your little town and that will make life a bit easier. What d'you say it's called?"

"Needful," Spencer said. "Just like all of us."

"Good luck Spencer," the Marshall said, with a wave as the younger man swung into the saddle and turned away.

Spencer spurred his horse into a trot as he left the edge of town. They would all be trail weary before they reached Needful, but they could rest at the end of the ride. He was going home. Home to his son and home to his heart.

Chapter 23

Daliah walked to the edge of town under the watchful gaze of Dan Gaines. In the past few weeks, it had become a ritual that each evening, as the sun was setting behind her, Daliah would watch at the edge of town, gazing over the prairie and scanning for any signs of Spencer.

It had been nearly a month and a half since Dan had returned from Dallas and had taken up his watchful care over his brother's betrothed.

A full moon hung low in the sky as the golden rays flashed their last light across the green prairie and Daliah sagged with disappointment as no sign of a lonely rider could be seen.

Ever since Dan had received the telegram stating that Daliah had been cleared and that Spencer was on his way home, she had watched, anticipating his return, but once again, the day ended without the better part of her heart coming home.

Turning, she took a step toward Dan, just catching the hint of movement to the North. Then, whirling, she stepped further out onto the grass, her heart pounding as a rider topped the nearest rise, a string of mules trailing behind.

Dan Gaines jumped to attention when Daliah stepped out onto the prairie. Had she seen something?

Grabbing his horse, he swung into the saddle, his eyes scanning the darkening sky as an inky silhouette caught his keen gaze, and he raced to catch up to Daliah, offering her a hand and pulling her up behind him on his horse, as they raced out to meet the arrival.

"It's him," Daliah said, clinging to Dan as he raced across the trail. "I know it's Spencer," she cried.

Dan pulled rein in front of his brother a few moments later, barely able to keep Daliah from falling off the horse as she dropped to the ground only to be swept up into Spencer's strong arms. His feet hit the earth.

"You're here," Daliah sobbed, burying her face in his shoulder as she clung to him.

"I'm here, darlin', I'm here," he crooned, looking up and offering his brother a nod of thanks.

Daliah looked up, pulling away from Spencer, her face flushed as she wiped the tears from her eyes, but Spencer didn't let her go.

"Good to see you made it back in one piece," Dan

said, leaning down and offering his brother his hand. "Look a little the worse for wear, though," he added with a chuckle rubbing his chin in imitation of Spencer's ragged beard.

Spencer's sharp bark of laughter didn't even garner a raised head from his weary stock. "I might have pushed it a bit," he agreed, then looking down at Daliah added, "it was worth it, though."

Dan climbed down from his horse then hugged his brother. "You two go on," Dan said, handing the reins to his brother, his eyes taking in the joy on Spencer's face and wondering if he would ever have a woman look at him the way Daliah was looking at Spence. "I'll bring your stock."

Spencer helped Daliah up into the saddle in front of him, then swung up behind her, his eyes going to his brother in thanks. "I'll see you later," he said, itching to spur the fresh horse to where he knew his son would be.

"Is everyone doing well?" he asked instead as he turned the horse toward Needful. "The Hampton's, Chad?" he asked, his voice growing husky as he tightened his grip on Daliah.

"Everyone's fine," Daliah said. "We've been watching for you every day since Dan got the note."

It was only a matter of minutes before they were climbing down at the Hampton House, and even in the dim light, Spencer could see how much the place had changed.

The once simple structure was a full two-story building with oiled paper in the window openings and a front porch with a plank floor.

Helping Daliah down, he leaned forward, resting his forehead against hers. "I know you prayed every day for me," he said. "I could feel those prayers all the way in Missouri,"

Daliah closed her eyes, breathing in the smell of horse, trail dust, and Spencer himself. "I'm so thankful you're home," she whispered as he turned his head, dropping his lips to hers.

"Pa! Pa!" Chad burst from the front door, wrapping himself around Spencer's legs and squeezing tight.

Spencer leaned down, picking up his boy and hugging him. "You've grown," he said, his voice sounding gruff in his ears.

"It's all the good cookin'," the boy said, leaning back to run his hands over his father's dark beard then wrapping his arms around him again. "Are you home forever now?" the boy asked, holding on tight.

"Forever and ever," Spencer said, pulling Daliah closer as together they walked into the welcoming dining hall.

Chapter 24

"Pa, do I have to wear this?" Chad asked the following Sunday as his father pulled a string tie around the boy's collar.

"Yes, you have to wear the suit and the tie," Spencer said. "Today, Daliah is going to become my wife and your mother," he finished standing and adjusting the black tie around his collar. He grinned, checking to see that he'd shaved carefully enough. For some reason, Daliah hadn't cared much for his beard.

"Then we'll move into our house, right?"

"That's right," Spencer said.

"Then we'll build a jail in case bad people come to town."

Spencer chuckled. "You don't miss much, do you?" he said.

"Everyone's talking about it," Chad said. "Uncle Dan said you was gonna be the Sherriff."

Again Spencer chuckled. He didn't know how

he'd let his brother and the others of the town talk him into it, but he had agreed to be the Sheriff of their burgeoning town. He couldn't help but wonder if Tom Eagan had also had a hand in the nomination somehow, but it felt right.

"Well, the town had a need for a Sheriff," he admitted combing his hair down.

"Cause our town's Needful," Chad said, his blue eyes sparkling.

"That's right, son, and right now, we need to get ready before your new ma thinks we changed our mind."

Chad climbed up on a box and looked into the tiny mirror next to his father. "We look pretty good, don't we?" he said, sticking a finger in his collar and tugging slightly.

***

Daliah smoothed the dress she had put away so many weeks ago and tried to slow the flutter of her heart.

"You look beautiful," Mrs. Hampton sighed, clasping her hands as she stepped back from fixing Daliah's hair.

"You are beautiful," Rosa said, handing her a small bouquet of wildflowers. "It is our first Needful wedding," she added, adjusting Christine on her hip.

Daliah moved to the tiny woman wrapping her in her arms. "Won't Raoul be surprised when he returns from the cattle drive?" she asked, knowing that Rosa must be missing her husband more than ever today.

A soft knock fell on the door, and all three called for Mr. Hampton to come in. "You ready?" he asked, his eyes glowing with appreciation. "Your men are gettin' fidgety in there."

"I'm ready," Daliah said, gliding to the old man who had done so much for her and taking his arm.

In what felt like the blink of an eye, she stood hand in hand with Spencer before the preacher and said her vows while Chad fidgeted with the pillow that held the rings. It seemed like a dream to finally say the words that would bind them together for life.

As she repeated the word that tied her to Spencer, her heart filled with praise to a God who had never forsaken her and had worked for her good.

When the preacher pronounced them man and wife, and Spencer had sealed their love with a kiss, the whole town erupted in loud cheers as they welcomed the new couple as part of Needful Texas.

The party that lasted into the night solidified the growing kinship of the town that had changed so much, and as the wedding supper was served, the men turned to discuss changes that would come to their town.

"We'll need a mayor," Mr. Scripts said.

"What do we need a Mayor for," another man spoke up, "we already got Dan."

Laughter filled the dining hall, but others weren't done yet. "We already got a new Sheriff," another man said, "Not that he's got much lawin' to do yet, why not elect a Mayor as well."

"I nominate Dan Gaines!" someone in the back of the room called out.

"I second," someone else added their voices as Spencer took Daliah's hand and led her outside.

"I think Dan's about to become a town official," he said, letting the cool evening air wash over them as they escaped the overly full room.

"You think he'll accept?" Daliah asked, shivering slightly.

"I don't think he'll have much choice," Spencer said, lifting her fingers to his lips. "But that's his problem," he added. "For now, I'm taking my new bride to my new home and starting a new life."

"Daliah!" Chad burst from the Hampton House's front door, racing toward her, an excited grin on his face. "You forgot your hat," the boy said, skidding to a stop. He'd talked about nothing but the fact that he would be spending the night with Trey and the Scripts for the night, and his eyes sparkled with a clear blue light.

Daliah let go of Spencer's hand and pulled Chad into her arms. "I don't think I'll be needing that now," she said, taking the hat from the boy's small hands and smoothing the rumbled brim. "I think maybe you could keep it and take care of it for me," she added with a happy tear as she settled the hat on his head.

"You mean it?" Chad asked breathlessly, trying to look at the hat brim above him.

"I mean it," Daliah said. "I know you'll take good care of it and now that I have you and your father to love, I feel like this hat is ready to be of real use again."

Chad threw his arms around Daliah's neck, squeezing her tight. "I'm sure glad you married my pa," the boy said, stepping back and placing a hand over the hat as he bolted back to the festivities.

Epilogue

Spencer grabbed the young miscreant by the collar and tossed him into the wood slat cell, slamming the door home. "You can sleep it off in there," he said, as the man dropped onto the bunk with a loud belch.

Some men from the surrounding ranches seemed to have too much time on their hands recently, and he thought he might have a talk with the Mayor about the catcalls and whistles the decent women of the town had been subjected to lately. A new ranch had started up to the southeast, and the men there were unruly at best.

"That's the third one this week," Daliah said, stepping into the tiny office with a pot of coffee and a fresh mug. "I guess it's to be expected with so many single men in town."

"You've been talking to Olive again, haven't you," Spencer said, leaning in and taking the items from her with a quick kiss.

"She's right, Spencer," Daliah insisted. "If there were more women in town, the men might settle down a bit."

"You mean wives," Spencer said, filling the mug and walking back to the cell, placing it in the intoxicated man's hands.

"You have a wife and it doesn't seem to have done you any harm," Daliah teased. "Olive is just thinking about this town. I know it's a cow town, but the families that came here with you are trying to make something of it, and the Governor said that the rail would reach Dallas this winter. So that means more people will be arriving."

Spencer pulled Daliah into him as he perched on the desk, kissing her softly and laughing when she blushed.

"And how do you plan on getting single young women to come to our little town?" He asked.

"I don't know," Daliah admitted, "but Olive has something up her sleeve."

Spencer laughed. "I'll leave her to it then. We have a load of work that still needs done around here. We only just got the jail built, and from what Dan says, we'll see cold weather soon."

"I'm glad the Scripts have their store finished," Daliah mused. "It's still a little rough, and they don't have much in stock until Mr. Scripts goes back down to Galveston."

"Good thing I brought you all those nice things

for our house when I came home then, isn't it," Spencer teased.

"I can't believe all of the things you brought," Daliah said. "Every time I cook a meal or do the wash, I'm thankful."

Spencer leaned in, kissing her lips one more time. "You are way too easy to please," he said.

"I had no idea the day I was dismissed from the bank in Smithfield what it would lead to," Daliah said. "I have a home of my own, a rather hearty fix and stitch situation where I can help those in need, and am married to the world's most handsome sheriff," she finished with a bright smile.

"I can't say I saw that coming," Spencer admitted. "I'm just thankful that between working Dan's ranch and helping to keep the streets clear of trouble makers, I can provide for you and Chad. Where is he, by the way?"

"Chad is doing lessons with Ben," she said. "He's using our parlor today, but they've been discussing a school."

"Aren't many kids that need a school," Spencer mused, taking her hand and leading her out the door. "I never would have taken old Ben as the type to pick up teaching. Didn't even know he could read, for that matter," he added, closing the door and turning to walk home with his lovely wife.

Together they paused, gazing down the clean street of the town. On one end, the old saloon stood, the faint sound of a tinny piano drifting from its open doors. On the other end, the Hampton House stood tall and proud, ready to welcome newcomers with a brightly painted sign declaring good eats and rooms.

Their place was next door to the jail, and Daliah had plans to plant flowers and a spring garden.

"A lot fewer tents these days," Spencer said. "I can't believe what has been accomplished in this town already in just eight months."

"It's a Needful town," Daliah said, taking his arm, "but God can provide all our needs if we believe."

***

Olive rifled through the pages of the paper that had arrived in the mail, searching for a specific small brochure. "I know it's here somewhere," she grumbled, turning to look accusingly at some of the married women of Needful. "Ah, here it is," she called, waving it high. "I'll give you each a page and you see what you can find. We have a great need here in Needful, and I think this will be the best way to go about it."

Olive Hampton pulled the pages of the smaller issue apart, handing them to the three other women in her parlor.

"What do you want us to do with it?" Mrs. Scripts asked. "How are we supposed to get this done?"

"We'll each choose one of the needful and find a likely match," Mrs. Hampton said, settling in front of the quilting frame that had been lowered from the ceiling an hour earlier. "We'll all write letters and inquiries until we find one that fits the need, and then we'll pool our resources and bring them out."

The other women nodded their heads, peering down at the pages in their hands.

"I hope the train comes through in January like they's sayin' it will," one of the older women said. "It will make this whole enterprise much easier."

The End

Follow Me:

https://www.authordanniroan.com/

Next In Series:

Prim

Sneak Peek:

Prologue

"Peri, you have the most ridiculous notions about marriage," Primrose Perkins said as she shifted her berry pail from one hand to the other.

"You don't know," her sister Periwinkle said, wrinkling her nose at Prim. "You and me won't never get to fall in love, anyway. Pa'll see to it we stay home and tend ma forever."

Primrose shook her head of dark brown hair, her blue eyes growing soft. "I don't mind looking after Ma," she said. "I know you'd love to have a beau and think some fancy man is going to come whisk you away to a big house full of cakes and tea, but that don't happen in real life."

Peri stuck her tongue out at her older sister. "You are so serious," she chided. "I know my dreams are big, but at least I have some."

Primrose drew in a deep breath reaching across the prickly blackberry stalks to pluck the ripe fruit. "I'm only trying to be practical," she admitted. "I'm sure real romance would be thrilling, but I don't think it always works out like people hope. Look at Ma. She's next thing to a simpleton after that cow kick to the head, and Pa's not much account hiding from the law up here in the hills."

"But not everyone is like Pa," Peri insisted. "Ma must have loved him once, before that nasty cow stepped on her and took her away with the fairies. I can't imagine Mama would have married him the way he is now."

"Maybe," Prim admitted, "but I'm going to keep my head about the whole romance thing, and one day I'll get a job and do for myself. I don't need a man to love to be happy."

Peri dropped a handful of the deep purple berries into her own bucket and moved around the wild bushes, keeping her skirt clear of the clinging thorns. "Well I'm going to marry a fancy man and be happy forever," she sassed with a giggle. "I'll even take Ma to live with me, and she can sit in her old rocker and put the dozen or so babies I have to sleep each night."

Primrose laughed the sound winging across the breeze like bird song. "I hope it happens for you little sister. I want you to be happy."

"I plan on it," Periwinkle laughed giving her skirt a swish.

The sound of a shotgun blast made both girls turn toward home, their blue eyes going wide as another blast met their ears.

Grabbing her sister's hand Primrose dropped her bucket and began racing toward home her heart pounding in her breast.

***

Prim came to a stop at the edge of the bushes that surrounded the small cabin she shared with her family, and she gazed into the brighter light of the tiny clearing.

A sorry kitchen garden at the back of the squat log structure drooped in the warm Tennessee sun as she scanned the area for the commotion or danger.

"Prim," Peri sobbed covering her mouth with one hand even as she pointed toward the far side of the house with the other to where her father's moonshine still, sat puffing steam.

"Pa," Prim groaned stepping out onto the dirt yard and heading toward the two men who stood over her father's limp body. "What are you doing?" she cried her voice shrill with panic. "That's my father."

"He shot at us," a tall man with a droopy mustache said. "We didn't mean ta kill 'em, but he shot at us first."

"Who, who are you?" Peri asked dropping to her father's side and rolling him over only to take in his blank eyed stare. "Oh Pa," the girl moaned as tears spilled down her face.

"He shot first," the man repeated sadly looking down at Peri who was crying softly over her father.

"Ma," Prim cried turning and racing toward the door of the tiny cabin. "Mama?" she asked her voice high and shrill as she braced one hand on the door jamb and slid through the open door. "Mama, are you alright?"

Stepping into the darker interior of the cabin, Prim took in the familiar scene as her mother rocked back and forth in her old chair, her slightly drooping lips locked in a half smile.

"Mama," Prim said walking to the chair and kneeling before the woman in the faded dress. "Mama, Pa's dead," Prim said softly studying the other woman's eyes for understanding. "He's gone Mama," Prim repeated until the dark eyes met hers.

As Primrose studied her mother's vacant face, a soft humming of an old hymn was the only reaction Prim received from her mother as the old woman started rocking once more.

"Prim," Peri walked into the room still sniffling. "What are we going to do? Those men are revenuers."

"I don't know," Prim said rising and brushing off her skirts. "We'll have to find Pa's money and think of where Ma can go. You stay here while I go talk to them men," she finished stepping back out into the bright sunlight of a summer day.

"What's going to happen to us?" Primrose asked lifting her chin as she stared down the two lawmen who still stood over her father's lifeless body. Perhaps she was only the daughter of a lowly moonshiner, but she wasn't going to sit by and do nothing.

"I don't know miss," the younger of the two men said. "We'll take him back to town with us," he said nodding toward her father. "He'll get a decent burial. I promise."

"You girls and your ma can come back to town with us if you want," the older man said looking around at the sad living quarters. "You got kin anywhere?"

Prim clamped her hands together thinking. "I have an aunt in Rockington," she said. "Maybe she can take us in for a bit until we figure out what to do."

***

"Do we got everything?" Peri asked looking around the sad little cabin she had called home for the past eight years of her life.

Before her mother had been kicked in the head by a mean old cow, the Perkins family had lived in the little town of Rockington where Mr. Perkins had been employed at a tobacco farm. Unfortunately, without Ma to manage the money and keep her father going to work daily, everything had fallen apart.

"I think so," Prim replied looking around. Since the lawmen had taken their father away, they had harvested all of the vegetables they could from the garden, loaded the canned goods from the pantry, and packed up everything they could carry, in the rickety buckboard then hitched up the mule.

"I'll fetch Ma if you want to bring her chair," Peri offered looking around with a sniff. "I wouldn't ever have believed I would feel sad leaving this place," the younger woman said. "It just don't seem possible that Pa is gone."

Primrose wrapped an arm around her sister hugging her. "Let's go fetch the last of the blackberries before we go," she said, "Mama can rock for a few more minutes. We'll make more jam when we get to Aunt Betsy's place."

Peri looked up with a grin nodding as she fetched the pails from the wagon. One last walk in the forest they loved would be a good way to store up memories of their deep green mountain home.

Sign up for my Newsletter and get a free book!
Subscribe

If you enjoyed this book, check out more books by Danni Roan follow me on Facebook, Twitter, Bookbub

If you'd like to get updates on my work, see special sneak peeks and be entered in special contests sign up for my newsletter on my webpage.

For more amazing Western Historical Romance join me and my friends at Pioneer Hearts a facebook group for readers like you.

Dear Reader,

Thank you for choosing to read my book. I hope you have enjoyed it as much as I've enjoyed writing it. If you enjoyed the story, please feel free to leave a review wherever you purchased the book. Leaving a review will help me and prospective readers to know what you liked about this book. It is an opportunity for your voice to be heard and for you to tell others why the story is worth a read.

About the Author

Danni Roan, a native of western Pennsylvania, spent her childhood roaming the lush green mountains on horseback. She has always loved westerns and specifically western romance and is thrilled to be part of this exciting genre. She has lived and worked overseas with her husband and tries to incorporate the unique quality of the people she has met throughout the years into her books. Although Danni is a relatively new author on the scene, she has been a story teller for her entire life, even causing her mother to remark that as a child "If she told a story, she had to tell the whole story." Danni is truly excited about this new adventure in writing and hopes that you will enjoy reading her stories as much as she enjoys writing them.

Other Books in this Series

Brides of Needful Texas

Daliah

Prim

Peri

Beth

Ruth

Amanda

Adele

Fanny

Olga

Heidi

About The Author

Danni Roan

Danni Roan, a Christian author, has always been a storyteller and that unique talent has translated well into the western romance genre. Danni's characters are real, genuine and come alive on the page. To date, Danni has two  western romance series, The Cattleman's Daughters and Tales from Biders Clump, as well as several stand-alone novellas in the Strong Hearts: Open Spirits group. Danni has also participated in several multi-author projects including Whispers in Wyoming, a Christian, Contemporary Western Romance series and the much anticipated Alphabet Mail-Order Brides series.

Danni has Bachelors of Missiology and a Masters in Teaching English as a Second Language (ESL). Danni has taught English and ESL, for over fifteen years both overseas and at home in the United States. These skills and her experience with people from all over the world have given a special flavor to her writing which only adds to the authenticity of her characters.

Danni lives with her every-day-hero of more than twenty-seven years in a thirty-six-foot camper that they are using to tour the United States, adding new life to the setting and drama of her books. She is very proud of their son who is studying at the University of Florida. You can follow Danni's adventures on her blog as well as reading about them in her work.

Danni is a member of the Pioneer Hearts Authors and Readers group on facebook and loves working with and interacting with so many talented friends. She has made lasting connections and feels that she is a part of something bigger than herself.

Originally hailing from Pennsylvania Danni feels a connection to the land and loved riding over the verdant hills of western PA on horseback throughout her youth.

Made in the USA
Coppell, TX
21 November 2021

66113089R00132